IRENEC PRINCIPLE

Fiction: the Precursor of Fact

Alan Roderick-Jones

PUBLISHED BY FIDELI PUBLISHING, INC.

Original Story by Alan Roderick-Jones

Based on a screenplay by
Alan Roderick-Jones and Robert Joseph Aloha

Technical Advisor: Charles Stevens. (Livermore)

Dedication

Rachel, Ella, and Rowan
Always there with unconditional love
your hearts, your understanding,
You are there within my eternal heart

For those who choose the stillness within
and
walk the path of gentleness
carrying light in their wake

Gratitude for initial creative input:
Charles Eric and Brian Christopher Johnson

Table of Contents

Preface ix

Author's Note............................. xi

ONE — Release me from this earth 1

TWO — How we postulate our universe 7

THREE — Total Eclipse 11

FOUR — Earth dealt her harshest blow 16

FIVE — Assassination 2033 19

SIX — Mist and rain 22

SEVEN — Echoes across empires 28

EIGHT — The weight of morning...................... 33

NINE — The shape of shadows..................... 37

TEN — The weight of light............................. 40

ELEVEN — Shadows and still water 46

TWELVE — The edge beyond knowing.................... 52

THIRTEEN — Ancient ley lines........................ 56

FOURTEEN — The storm before.................... 60

FIFTEEN — The river remembers 65

SIXTEEN — The veil is lifting 70

SEVENTEEN — The light that listens..................... 76

EIGHTEEN — Jade Spring Hill, Beijing 81

NINETEEN	The arrival	84
TWENTY	The oval and the edge	90
TWENTY-ONE	What's happening?	94
TWENTY-TWO	The middle of the riddle	98
TWENTY-THREE	The cold geometry of trust	103
TWENTY-FOUR	In the shadows and on the shores	106
TWENTY-FIVE	Ghosts in the code	111
TWENTY-SIX	Whale of a surprise	115
TWENTY-SEVEN	The birds have flown	118
TWENTY-EIGHT	Eternal essence	127
TWENTY-NINE	Profound science is wonder	133
THIRTY	The Rajdhani Express	141
THIRTY-ONE	The Knight's Gambit	146
THIRTY-TWO	The exchange	153
THIRTY-THREE	Peace, like power, is always leveraged	156
THIRTY-FOUR	The Irenic cylinders	162
THIRTY-FIVE	Lake Band-e Amir	168
THIRTY-SIX	The Irenic Principle	173
THIRTY-SEVEN	The threshold	177
THIRTY-EIGHT	Somewhere unseen	180
THIRTY-NINE	Irenic shield	186

Story Behind the Story: Acknowledgements and Reflections . 195

About the Author ... 199

Preface

THIS STORY BEGAN WITH A QUESTION: What if peace isn't merely a human aspiration, but a fundamental principle? Something woven into the very fabric of reality, waiting to be revealed? From that question emerged Dr. Jessica Peak, a physicist whose pursuit of truth leads her to the brink of a discovery with the power to reshape our understanding of ourselves and the universe.

Jessica's journey is one of science, but also of conscience. It is a search that unfolds in the quiet, often perilous space between knowledge and belief where the boundaries of fact and faith blur, and where the consequences of discovery reach far beyond the laboratory.

This novel is fiction, but the questions it raises are real: What if the forces that govern our world hold secrets about peace, connection, and consciousness that we have yet to imagine? What responsibilities come with such knowledge? And how might our beliefs change if we allow ourselves to see the universe differently?

I invite you to read with both curiosity and caution. The answers may surprise you, and the questions may linger long after the final page.

Alan R-J

Author's Note

At the time of this writing, nine nations are widely believed to possess nuclear weapons: the United States, Russia, the United Kingdom, France, China, India, Pakistan, North Korea, and Israel. Notably, Israel maintains its long-standing policy of ambiguity, neither confirming nor denying its nuclear status—a stance that quietly shapes regional and global conversations alike.

As this story is set in the year 2033, I added one more country

with

a

nuclear arsenal:

Turkey

Irenic (adjective)

Derived from the Greek word *eirēnē,* meaning "peace especially in the face of conflict or division."

IRENEC PRINCIPLE

Fiction: the Precursor of Fact

ONE

Release me from this earth

Soar with each precious moment,
for you know not which given breath will be your last.

LIGHT RADIATES. A DAZZLING OCEAN. Translucent waves pulse through my being. Submerge me in your tranquil water. Draw me closer to your radiant surface. I break through.

There is a calming stillness. A soft, tender voice calls. I know this feeling, it's so familiar. Release me from this Earth. My arms are raised. My body is so light. I'm rising. Flying, higher and higher. How fast the earth passes beneath me. Swiftly now, low over fields of wheat. The poppies are so red. The blue cornflowers vibrant.

The gentle voice still calls across the mountain river, through the tall pines. *Up. Up. Into the light.*

How glorious I feel, swooping down the crest of a waterfall, into the depths of the mountain and up to the snow-covered peaks. The snow is turning red. Red, like the soil of my valley. The mountain is cascading into the river.

Where is the light?

1

I hear an anguished cry. A child is crying. He is there. There, in the light. He is all alone. I cannot see his face. A child named Asha cries, "Mummy!"

"Mummy, please don't leave me!" a frightened Asha cries again.

Why is he holding out his arms to me? I cannot help him. I am helpless.

Where is he? Don't go. He's fading. Asha, please stay.

There is a figure there behind him. Another and another. Three. I know them all. *Please stay with me. I will never leave you, Asha.*

I am so scared. Why are they all leaving me?

In the bleak, dusty gray murk of pre-dawn, two eyes blink open to stare through a black void. They struggle for a moment with the darkness, then drift and focus, gazing through a haze of ashen cobwebs that hang under a black, soot-filled ceiling. Like remnants of ghosts, the silk threads haunt the phantom shadows above Krista's head.

Beads of cold sweat drip from her forehead. The drenched strands of her coarse hair cling to her moist cheek and neck. Krista's beauty wasn't in her Nordic-boned features, but in the feminine magnetism that exuded from her very presence. Her weather-toned face was framed by long, prematurely graying auburn hair. Her deep blue eyes were truly the mirror of Krista's life journey.

She was thirty-nine. War had taken its toll, and she looked forty-five. In bare feet, she was no more than five foot three inches tall. The Hollywood actress Anna Magnani could have easily been the reflection that gazed back at her from the broken mirror on the stone wall.

She was like a mountain wildcat sparring with its prey—agilely twisting, turning, then going for the kill. In the past years of chaos, her tongue became an arrow of defense in flight, aiming directly for the bullseye of human targets—the Russian adversary. She would come to her family's defense, disarming many a terrifying situation with feminine charm, tenacity, and a word well-placed.

Lying motionless, Krista swallows to relieve the dry, choking feeling in her throat as she desperately strains to recall the dream. Remembering again, her breath quickens; she exhales short, shallow, asthmatic breaths. She releases the emotional tension by pressing her fingers into the corners of her eyes.

Softly, she questions, "Asha? Asha?"

She removes her hands and, in a heartbeat, throws aside the coarse sheepskin bedcovers. Taking three bounds across the cold slab granite floor, Krista clasps the rail of the simple wooden cot, hesitates, chokes out a sigh of relief, and looks down upon her sleeping three-year-old son.

With one leg hanging out of the rail, Asha had obviously outgrown his cozy nest. Krista gently places his foot back under the cover, touches his soft gypsy-red hair, and with a sigh, leans in closer to whisper:

"Asha, it was just a dream. Thank God, it was only a dream."

Catching a glimpse of herself in the small cracked mirror, Krista shivers as a chill travels up her spine. She looks across to the window, bows her head, and clasps her hands to her breast to pray.

"Help me understand," she pleads. She looks across at Asha.

"I love him more than life. Please don't take him from me. Haven't I suffered enough?" Her hands enfold the rail of the crib. If she'd had the strength this time, the old wood would have snapped from the intensity of her selfless desire.

"Take me instead," she says.

She carefully tucks the covers in around his little body and holds her hand in the warmth of his armpit. There are no words that could ever explain what she felt for her only surviving son. In her deep, heartfelt emotion were the fading images that the night had given her. Asha was a beautiful gift.

Krista crosses slowly to the small casement window set deep into the thick stone walls. She grasps the latch. The cracked skin of her knuckles awakens a memory of childhood tenderness. Krista remembers how soft her hands were then.

She opens the window and gazes out across the damp morning mist to the ghostly image of a now NATO tank, not like the Russians though. The tip of the cannon points directly at her, reminding Krista of her father's accusing forefinger, his gesture that would jab at her from the darkness of his aging solitude.

Krista mutters softly, "Will they never leave?"

She quickly closes the window and rubs the sole of her small left foot against the back of her calf for warmth. She continues to mutter under her breath.

"There's no rush. The sun isn't up yet. I'll lie down a little longer and then light the fire. I miss the cockerels. They always used to wake me. Now dead, they are all gone." An angry tone enters her voice. She flicks her hair out of her eyes, looks beyond the walls, and says:

"All eaten by those pitiful men. They were always too stringy anyway."

Wiping her neck dry with the collar of her nightdress, she looks sadly around her small, dismal room and slides back under the warmth and security of her covers. Krista bolsters her pillows and pulls the top sheet up under her chin. She cherishes these few moments with her silent thoughts before Asha wakes up.

She lets her knees fall and lays back into the comfort of the goose down that molds securely around her head. Glancing lovingly across to Asha, Krista lets her eyes drift to the window. The condensation on the inside of the glass and the morning frost outside become a trigger to her past memories. As she stares through, then out and beyond the glass, it all becomes a blurred haze.

She unconsciously drifts back, back to her childhood.

Spring's first touch filled my heart with joy, when the fields in the valley were carpeted with wildflowers. Now I feel like a winter's day, longing for the warmth of spring to melt the snow to change the skeleton trees to leafy pillows of green.

The summer days were filled with the laughter of my younger sister, Helena, and my brothers, Josh and Keela. Those wonderful balmy days in the fields of long, sweet-smelling grass. The wild daffodils were my favorite. I loved their delicate smell and lying in the grass with Keela, playing angels, and sucking the juices from a wheat shaft. So warm and golden.

The sycamore seeds with their angel wings would spiral down through the still air. The blue sky spectrums through with perfection to night. Stars would travel across the heavens. The moon became our lantern, lighting a path home to the security and the comfort of bed.

We lived in a timeless world. Paddled barefoot in the shallows of the fast-flowing, cold mountain river. Sat on the old grandfather tree that fell the day Father died. A lightning bolt split the tree in two, conveniently creating a bridge for us to cross the river.

We no longer had to run along the river's edge through the dappled light of the tall poplar trees to the old stone bridge. We could cross. Father loved to fish from that bridge.

Somehow, I don't remember being sad when Father died.

But I cried for days when Keela drowned. He looked so cold when they pulled him from the river.

A teardrop slowly pushes its way from under her eyelid to roll down her cheek. Krista opens her mouth to catch it with the tip of her tongue, awakening to eyes filled with tears. She bites the inside edge of her lip, sniffs, and allows her tears of love and loss to flow, remembering, for a brief moment, her two sons, Isher and Keelab.

I begged him not to take them. "It is for the cause," Jakra had said. How stubborn Jakra was.

Then she turns on her side, pulls the sheets around her, and clutches them tightly to her chest. Her lips part, but she does not speak. She doesn't have to dig too deep to pull from her stream of consciousness.

That moment in time she wonders, *Could I hold onto it for eternity?*

When I stood in the doorway of the cottage and watched all three of them disappear over the brow of the dell below, I had that instinctive notion that only mothers have. My Isher knew, because he turned and waved. I know he somehow knew, and then I knew I would never see them all again.

She swallows her sorrow. "Why?" Krista mouths the words. "Why did they have to go with their father?"

It was a short week. Strange how those days, all seven of them, suddenly seemed like they would never pass. They rolled into one desperate knowing. The hungry young man, caked in mud, brought her the devastating news that they had been killed by a Russian air attack.

She places her hand across her mouth to muffle the cry. "Oh God! If you are there how could you take my life?" She sits up and sighs.

"I felt like a single stem of wheat that had lost its husks before ripening. The dawn that forever lives within its mists, never to see sunlight. They were my life, not their father. Yes, I loved him, but I pulled my children out with my fingers." She smooths down the bedcover to touch an old fading bloodstain.

TWO

How we postulate our universe

AB BARIK WAS THE NAME of a small mountain village, comprised of eight moderately sized stone dwellings with grass and peat roofs. They nestled in the shelter of monolithic rocks, granite sentinels that had stood unmoved for millennia, guarding the hardened descendants of this rugged land. Eight generations of Afghan mountain folk had lived here, their very souls honed by the harsh and unforgiving weather that blasted bitter winter winds through to the marrow. Like the stone monoliths themselves, the family Krista had married into had endured, standing their ground through time and turmoil.

Fifty-four years ago, the Russian soldiers first came threading their way through the high peaks of the Badakhshan Mountains. They came, they killed, they raped, and they left. Now they were back. Twelve young NATO rookies and one officer, just a border patrol doing their duty. Frightened strangers in a hostile, war-torn land, they struggled to breathe in the thin mountain air.

From the remains of two dilapidated buildings blown apart in the initial onslaught, the soldiers now had cobbled together a crude shelter against the bitter cold. A canvas tent, tied down over the ruins, served as a makeshift roof. The well-worn goatskin flap parted as the officer stepped out into the morning's cold embrace. He pulled his tunic tighter and fumbled with the buttons on his trousers. His fingers were already numb from the chill. Sniffing the air, he glanced up at the mountains towering behind him. Melted snow trickled over the rocks, winding through narrow crannies to join a fast-flowing mountain stream, beginning its arduous journey to reunite with its source.

The officer turned to face the hillside that flanked the stream to the east. Unbuttoning his fly, he stepped behind the tank to take his first piss of the day. The soft glow of the rising sun broke through the summit of the cloud-covered peaks, creating shards of white light that sliced across the mist like slivers of frosted glass.

At first, it looked like a large gnat. Within seconds, it became a soaring bird. Then came a shrill whine that ripped through the village as an upgraded Su-75 Stealth fighter tore through the low cloud cover, missing the rooftops by mere feet. Still urinating, the officer dropped to the ground in shock, wetting his pants and cursing loudly. "Bloody Russians. Still at it!"

Asha woke up screaming.

Sparks flew up the stone chimney as a log cracked in the flames. The sound of the jet had pierced Krista's heart as sharply as it had startled the officer. She ran from the fire to Asha's cot, lifting the frightened boy into her arms.

"*Awlad Khar* (son of a donkey), you bastards!" she cursed, raising her fist to the ceiling. Then, softening, she kissed Asha's forehead gently.

The firewood tumbled from the hearth. She kicked it back into the ashes. There was barely any wood left in the area to burn. Painful, exhausting trips down the mountain to the valley, basket slung across her back only allowed for a small fire twice a week. But today, she decided, was as good an excuse as any.

With Asha perched on her hip, Krista passed through the hand-woven blanket that separated her life from that of her mother-in-law, Shad. She had never truly loved this woman. Though Krista had been accepted into her husband's family, they had always kept her at a distance. She wasn't one of them. She was from the valley. They were mountain folk—hard-bred, their pores steeped in smoke, their hands chiseled from the earth's anvil. Krista was soft-skinned, pale—a river woman.

Shad was ninety today. Fragile and wizened, her skin hung from her bones like worn leather. Krista moved quietly across the stone floor to a dark corner of the room. A small, high window in the north-facing wall offered the only light, casting a cold gray hue across the space. As Krista reached for the woman's soiled clothes, Shad stirred, sniffed, and coughed up phlegm. She spat it out unconsciously.

Krista turned her head in disgust, muttering to herself, "'Til death do us part, she'll outlive us all." She couldn't help but laugh softly. "Thank God she's still asleep," she added, hurrying from the room to drop the clothes into a small galvanized bath.

She placed Asha on the well-worn goatskin rug in front of the dim fire. "I'll make her curd for lunch. She'll like that," Krista said aloud. "Asha, your father would have liked that too."

She smiled, lost in the memory of Jakra and the laughter and joy he had brought into her life. His body had been strong and toned. How handsome he looked the day he shaved off his beard. He always nicked the same spot just under his nose, on the upper lip where a small mole hid. That's why he let the hair grow. A gentle lover, aggressive in his passion, he always wanted to please her, always brought her to the edge before himself.

But when the war broke out, something in him changed. He lost his passion for the earth, for family, for kin. Within a year, his hair had turned gray. He had grown distant. He would walk the mountains with the other men, grenades at their belts, rifles and anti-aircraft missiles slung across their shoulders. They looked like boys playing soldiers. Krista stayed behind to care for the children.

Then came the day he took them, her sons, and never returned.

What would he say now? she wondered, *if he could see the young NATO soldiers talking to his nieces?* Perhaps his sons would have been among them, slinking off into the hills, chasing youth's passionate release.

Asha had long forgotten the frightening sound of the jet and was now spitting out the curd Krista tried to spoon into his mouth.

"You're getting too old for me to feed you like this, Asha," she said, her patience thinning. She gave up on the bitter-tasting curd and handed him a crust of stale black bread to chew on. Then, bundling him up against the cold, she opened the door.

The wind swept through the room, stirring dust and cobwebs into sudden life. A few particles broke free from the roof and floated down like ash. Krista picked up the small bath and cradled it on her hip as the cat poked its nose around the doorframe. Asha, still clutching the bread, reached for his mother's free hand. She leaned into the wind, bracing herself.

Krista looked up at the sky. It was unusually dark, an eerie, foreboding shade that suggested a whole day had passed her by.

"If my eyes aren't deceiving me... wasn't that a star?" she whispered, bewildered. "At this time of day?"

She tightened her grip on Asha's hand as they stepped out to face the day, Asha with eyes wide in wonder, Krista with quiet trust.

How we postulate our universe...let us stretch the limits. Let the hidden library within us break open its seal. Let us be in awe of what life has in store.

THREE

Total Eclipse

IN ONE INFINITESIMAL CORNER of the vast ocean of space, a small companion sphere, Earth's astronomical partner, the Moon orbited at over 1,900 miles per hour, casting its shadow across the majestic face of its mutual gravitational attraction: our planet. A total eclipse of the Sun unfolded.

Just like a mirrored ball in a glass dance hall reflecting a powerful laser beam into a cavorting crowd, the Moon, with its illuminated side facing the Sun, cast a brilliant light. That light struck a small metal plaque riveted to a satellite locked in orbit around what humans often call "the dark side of the Moon."

There were no telltale emblems of NASA, and no country flags adorned this satellite, only the initials 'J.P' and a single word, IRENIC, engraved into its gleaming gold surface.

A soft mechanical whirl emitted from the depths of the satellite. The ignition of two small jets propelled the craft forward, releasing it from the Moon's gravitational pull and guiding it into a closer, more intimate orbit with Earth.

Beneath a small dish and antenna, both attached to a gold-painted metal truss, sat a Maksutov–Cassegrain telescope. Using a two-mirror system to gather and focus light with a correcting lens at the aperture and a curved secondary mirror. It revealed remarkable details of Earth's surface. The weight of the telescope had been significantly reduced by shortening its normal size by four-fifths.

But the eye to this instrument wasn't human. It was a finely crafted piece of ground-polished glass: a 1,500-millimeter lens with an extension. Focusing the high-definition camera, encased in a sheaf of gold leaf foil, was a motorized zoom that tracked forward and back along titanium rods.

The small cogs began to turn… the zoom disk rotated. Far below, a range of mountains in northwestern Asia, longitude 70.95, latitude 37.75 was struck by the sun's radiant energy as the Moon released its shadow from the Earth.

A red light atop the camera case flashed on. The lens found its focus. The small mountain border village of Ab Barik became its point of attention. The only sound in that celestial space came from the lens, as its operator somewhere on Earth continued to align it.

Eight stone dwellings came into view first. The camera drifted through the village's empty spaces before locking onto a group of young soldiers leaning against a tank. The markings indicated it was these were NATO troops.

Only twenty yards from the tank, a jeep was parked on a slope. A machine gun was mounted where the back seat would normally be. Leaning across the nozzle was a young soldier, sharing a moment of laughter with a local teenage girl.

The lens from space panned right and zoomed in. The girl looked nervous. She shyly twisted the long, single plait of her hair. Her smile personified youth in all its innocence.

Next, the lens panned across the village to find an old man with a thick, gray, nicotine-stained mustache standing on a worn stone threshold. The camera continued to pan, locating a mountain stream.

To the left, a woman knelt by the water's edge, washing clothes. At that moment, a small boy entered the frame from below. He picked up a stone and tossed it into the water in front of the woman. Startled, she looked up.

The camera zoomed in tighter. She wasn't looking at the boy. Her mouth opened in a silent scream.

In the same instant, she turned, dropped the garment she had been washing, and splashed across the stream, arms outstretched toward the child. But she did not reach him.

Her body twisted, then rose slightly before collapsing from the impact of a bullet that tore into her left shoulder blade. Her right arm moved forward, instinctively trying to break her fall. Instead, she fell face-down into the water.

Panning right, the frame filled with an explosion of dirt as a mortar shell struck the ground. Whoever was operating the lens reacted in shock. The camera lost focus.

A quick pan left then a 45-degree jerk down to the right. The lens refocused on the woman lying in the stream, lifeless, as the earth showered down on her.

The young boy, also covered in dirt, sat on the riverbank with his legs wide open, crying uncontrollably as he looked down at the woman. Beside him lay the remains of what may have once been a galvanized bath.

Again, the lens went out of focus. Then it refocused as it swept across the village, quickly settling on four young soldiers. They were panicked, running into a ruined building. Moments later, they reappeared, loading their rifles on the move. One soldier recoiled and fell back into a hanging animal skin. A shell obliterated the area on impact.

The camera tracked two of the remaining soldiers as they took shelter behind the tank. The tank skidded sideways across a rock outcrop, moved forward, and smashed into a stone wall. The roof of a small building collapsed as the tank crashed through it.

An old woman, upon seeing the oncoming tank, let out a silent scream as her frail body was crushed along with her bed.

A mortar shell blew a hole in the side of the building. The gunner, standing in the turret of the tank, was killed instantly by a large flying rock.

The red light on the satellite flashed on and off. The telescope's focal rim turned. The camera relocated.

A small band of Afghan rebels advanced over the brow of a hill. One knelt as another loaded a shell into a rocket launcher. It fired.

The camera followed its trajectory. The jeep exploded upon landing.

The young soldier who had been talking to the teenage girl lay dying, clinging to the machine gun as it continued to spew shells into the air. The girl lay dead in a smoldering crater, her body resembling a pale-skinned porcelain doll, her hair unkempt, as though awaiting a comb.

The camera panned down and continued right, locating the officer being attacked by two rebels. They tumbled down a steep slope into the shallow stream.

The older rebel tried to drown the officer by holding his head underwater. Gasping for air, the officer broke free and pulled out his bayonet just as the second rebel slashed him across the throat.

At that very instant, the lens zoomed in on the bayonet.

The molecular structure of the blade began to break down. The bayonet disintegrated.

The three men broke away from each other, stupefied.

They looked on in horror as their own bodies began to fracture into thousands of particles. Their vanishing faces mirrored their personal terror as the particles of matter simply disappeared into the air.

The camera tracked across the empty ground to a pool of blood flowing from the dead woman's body into the stream. Her body, too, was disintegrating into molecules of light.

A fallen, wounded rebel looked on in horror as the missile launcher he held fractured, disappeared, then reappeared only to vanish again.

The camera zoomed out to the boundary of the area. A high-intensity light began to form in the center of the village.

At first, a soft blue aura surrounded every person and object, whether stationary or moving. The blue light expanded until it encompassed everything.

A pulsating, radiant light emanated from its center. All that it touched became translucent.

The commander of the rebels, attempting to flee the outer limits of the wave, suddenly became airborne. He was swept back by a powerful wind into the central whirlpool of brilliance.

His body's molecular structure broke down into particles of light along with every other physical object, animate and inanimate.

The light vanished without a trace.

The dwellings were no longer there, once a village now an unearthly stillness.

The camera continued to roll, searching beyond the limits of the devastated arena. It panned across the stream, up the bank, and beyond, searching.

The iris on the camera closed. The zoom lens returned to its original position. The red light on the mount turned off.

The rockets of the satellite fired up, propelling The Witness to the earthly drama back into hiding behind the Moon's dark side.

The stage had been set.

<u>FOUR</u>

Earth dealt her harshest blow

DEATH BY ASSASSINATION MAY seem a premature calling card for those who knowingly choose to come to Earth for only a brief term to kindle a spark in the hearts of man.

The gray steel sky served as a silent messenger of the coming storm. Low, dark charcoal clouds, shaped like samurai warriors encircling a doomed enemy fortress, loomed above. They were heavy, their depths swollen with a deluge meant solely for the silent, suffering thirst of the ancient oaks, those quiet sentinels, that had once again survived yet another drought.

You could smell it. Feel its presence with every fiber of your being. Its approach stirred the senses, awakening them from the depths to which they had long been imprisoned. Anticipation. A knowing. The raw power of one of life's most sacred elements was about to be witnessed once again. Water. Immaculate. Falling from above.

A brisk wind tore through the trees, slicing the air and piercing their boughs, which swayed in submission to its force. A flock of crowing rooks, startled from their roost, took flight just as the storm made its presence known.

16

The first drop struck a leaf, then another, and another still. The earth, dry and cracked, was eager to drink them in. The rain came in an opaque sheet, a torrential downpour flooding the parched acres surrounding a red brick mansion in upstate New York.

Then, like an uninvited intruder, a gunshot rang out cracking through the thick air. A dark, fluttering object spiraled silently down in the rain.

The weather had always been taken for granted. Most pedestrians expected it to rain. Why not? Hadn't it always? The yearly average rainfall had exceeded five inches, at least in the northern regions of America. But those gifted with even a hint of awareness, whose voices were often dismissed with contempt felt a grim sense of validation as the forbidding crisis became more apparent.

Earth's signals circled her circumference. If you knew how to crack the code, it was clear: Mother Earth was angry. And yet, she was continually ignored, dismissed by the majority with apathetic indifference.

The heat intensified. El Niño events in the Pacific triggered droughts and claimed thousands of lives in Indonesia. In the summer of 1995, five hundred elderly people perished in a stifling heatwave that struck an unprepared, unsuspecting Chicago. Hurricanes devastated the entire North American coast. In 1998, tornadoes wreaked havoc across small communities in Alabama, leaving horror and despair in their wake.

Floods swelled rivers beyond any previously recorded heights. The waters broke free from their banks, ballistic and unrestrained. Homes and lands were consumed. The now unpredictable weather extended into winter, creating a hidden, silent despair.

With no compassion for her inhabitants, the Earth dealt her harshest blow yet. Freezing winds from the northern hemisphere drove chill factors to their lowest recorded levels. The subtle shift of tectonic plates had created a vast, frozen geophysical landscape:

but that didn't seem to bother the pimps and whores blowing bubbles in Times Square on New Year's Eve, their breath and laughter instantly turning to ice.

Who cared if it was fifty degrees below freezing? Wasn't it 2029?

Ring out the old. Bring in the new. Another opportunity. Another year to clean up the act.

Then came yet another drought.

Month after month passed in anticipation, hoping for the faintest breeze that might bring a single cloud. Just one. Then, perhaps, the parched earth would once again grow its carpet of succulent grass.

We wished.

On the digital readout perched above the L.A. Hard Rock Café, the planet's suicide level kept pace with the devastation of the world's forests. Man, in his solitude, was gripped by silent panic. He could no longer even rely on the seasons.

Finally, the Earth began to show signs of compassion.

No! I retract that.

Shedding painful tears of rejection, Mother had begun to cry.

FIVE

Assassination 2033

A DARK GREEN STRETCH MERCEDES 560 barrels dangerously fast through the narrow country lanes, racing toward its destination, the Manor House. But now, under the weight of a torrential downpour, the car slows to a tortoise's pace. The windscreen wipers are useless, the glass smeared and overwhelmed by the deluge.

Trevor, the chauffeur, curses under his breath. He wipes his hand across the inside of the windscreen, but it does little to improve visibility. Frustrated, he turns his head slightly, speaking to the passenger in the rear seat. "I'm sorry, sir," he says, apologizing for the weather. As he turns his eyes back to the road, he glances into the rearview mirror and catches the angry reflection of his passenger, Vice President Mallory.

"Who would have expected such a downpour, sir?"

But Mallory doesn't respond directly. Instead, a black-gloved finger presses the button that raises the glass partition between them. His snide voice cuts through just before the divide seals him off, "It surprises me, Trevor, that you even think."

Mallory's pallid, unshaven face is drawn tight with tension. His every mannerism betrays an invisible pressure. He leans forward and turns up the volume on the small flat-screen TV embedded in the panel before him. The screen flickers, revealing a concerned CNN anchor who interrupts the second semifinal of the NCAA Final Four with breaking news:

"There has been an assassination attempt on the President."

Mallory jerks upright. *"What?"* he exclaims, fury rising in his voice as the climactic sports moment is stolen from him and replaced by dread.

The anchor, oblivious to the collective disappointment of basketball fans across the country, continues with solemn gravity.

"At this hour, the President is resting safely, having survived a six-hour operation to remove four bullets from his body. Doctors report a fifty-fifty chance of recovery. His condition is currently stable. The assassin is still at large. Due to security risks, we cannot release further information. We at CNN pray for the President's speedy recovery."

"Shit! That bastard...idiot," Mallory mutters with tightly restrained rage.

He pulls off a glove, lowers the TV volume, and retrieves a compact phone from his coat. From another pocket, he produces a voice mute, which he attaches to the mouthpiece before dialing rapidly.

On the screen, CNN replays the harrowing footage in slow motion, frame by frame, as the President collapses from the podium, his body twisting with each bullet's impact.

Mallory grinds his molars, his frustration nearing eruption. When he speaks, his voice is distorted, cold, and laced with menace. "There will be no payment until you finish what we set out to do... Incompetence is not acceptable. You understand my gist? You'll hear from me later. Do not try to make contact. Understand?"

He doesn't wait for a reply. He ends the call and removes the voice mute with slow, deliberate motions. A sudden scratch of a tree branch dragging along the car's roof and rear window makes him recoil.

Thunder crashes, echoing through the car like a warning. Mallory's anger boils over.

"Bastard! Such incompetence! What a bumbling, incompetent bastard."

His eyes, now glassy with rage, he checks his wrist for the time, and slides the glass partition back down.

Trevor turns slightly. "Sir?"

He reacts to the word "Bastard" as it slips from Mallory's lips and slurs into a venomous command.

"Trevor, get this car and us out of this mess. We are late, and they have no patience for those who are not punctual. In fact, they hate it."

Trevor shrugs nervously and asks, "They, sir? We'll float there if we have to, won't we, sir? We were almost there before it started to rain. It can't be far. Right, sir?"

Mallory pulls his glove back on and stares into the liquid obscurity outside, unable to find a single point of focus.

Trevor leans into the steering wheel and accelerates.

"Pity they had to interrupt the game. My money was on Kentucky," Trevor says, speaking to the rearview mirror. "I thought they might panic as the game got close, they do at times, but not enough to sway the outcome. I hope they won."

He fiddles with the radio dials. "Can't pick up one station on the radio. This bloody weather." He mumbles on, tapping his fingers unconsciously to the rhythm of the rain drumming against the metal shell of the car.

Mallory, restless and deaf to Trevor's ramblings, slumps deeper into the leathered corner of his seat. His mind drifts ahead to the Manor House, already crafting excuses for the assassin's failure. He turns slightly, sensing the presence of a travel companion, a shadow of forbidding that he briefly acknowledges, then dismisses.

Under his breath, he mutters, "There's Peake... mustn't forget that one. Bitch."

A smile, amoral and chilling, curls in his mind's eye. He lifts a gloved finger and slowly traces it down the condensation spreading across the window.

SIX

Mist and rain

THE STORM CHURNS OVER the upstate New York countryside, its dark clouds bruised and roiling as dusk settles in. Lightning cuts across the sky in jagged sheets, briefly illuminating a few crows as they glide through the air, black silhouettes against the swirling, angry heavens. Wind howls through the bare branches of noble, swaying trees, carrying with it a chorus of foreboding.

Through the mist and rain, two blackout SUVs and the 560 Mercedes approach a narrow, weathered stone bridge that leads to a secluded, walled estate. The lead vehicle slows as it reaches a pair of rusted wrought-iron gates. After a brief inspection by a security guard, the gates creak open with mechanical precision. The convoy moves forward in unison, slicing through the downpour along a tree-lined drive.

On either side, chained Presa Canario hounds bark and strain at their leashes with ferocious pleasure, their massive frames barely contained. The vehicles come to a halt in front of a sprawling Tudor mansion, its stone façade glistening under the relentless rain.

Two attendants rush forward with umbrellas just as the rear door of the Mercedes opens. Vice President Douglas Mallory steps out. The driver, Trevor, awkwardly pushes through the attendants to help him with his coat, but Mallory brushes him off with a curt flick of the hand.

"A little late, Trevor. I won't be too long," Mallory mutters, irritation threading his voice. "Oh, and check out my old girl's damage," he adds as he runs a hand over the top of the car. "Bloody storm!"

Tall, lean, and now cloaked in his dark trench coat, he moves with the confidence of a man long past fearing storms. Rain sheets off his shoulders as he strides across the gravel, flanked by Secret Service agents holding umbrellas. He doesn't acknowledge the footman waiting to take his coat. He simply removes it with practiced grace and hands it off without a glance.

Inside, the mansion is all dark wood and shadows. One could easily imagine stepping back into the time of Henry VIII when entering this structure. Mallory's footsteps echo through the grand entrance hall as he walks slowly forward, a quiet tension settling over him. At the far end of the hall, an attendant opens a heavy door, revealing a large conference room.

The room is dim, lit only by the storm-filtered light seeping through tall windows, their heavy drapes partially drawn. It is silent, save for the soft hum of the holo-display flickering above the central oval oak table.

He has been summoned and he has arrived.

Here sit the most powerful beings on Earth…Or so they believe.

Mallory raises his arm, again checking the date and time on his Rolex 1945 Oyster Perpetual: November 10th, 2033. He takes a breath, steadying himself. Now, he must face *The Consortium.*

At the far end of the table sits a tall, silver-haired man, precise in both speech and manner. Director Malcolm Trent. An American who rarely shows emotion, though today his jaw is tight, his voice clipped. He has held this fragile alliance together for over a decade.

To his left, backlit by the storm-lit windows and opening a silver cigarette case, sits Sir Peter Murton, an English peer with a voice like a scalpel. Few words, but each one cuts deep.

Leaning toward the oscillating hologram at the center of the table is the French delegate, Minister Jean Rousseaux. His bulky frame and round belly speak of too many warm morning croissants and old-world indulgence.

Hovering above the table, four flickering holograms shimmer faces of light and shadow: a German industrialist, a Nigerian multibillionaire, a Japanese Yakuza don, and a Russian oligarch.

Mallory steps into the tall, beamed-ceilinged room, his expression unreadable. He pauses, eyes locking onto the man at the head of the table, older now, slightly hunched, but still wearing that same smug smile. Director Trent.

He hasn't changed, Mallory thinks, jaw tightening. *Still thinks he's untouchable. Still thinks I'm the scared kid who ran instead of fighting back.*

Trent smiles. "I was wondering when you'd show up through this storm," he says, gesturing toward the windows.

Mallory steps forward, voice calm, though his thoughts burn. *He doesn't know what I've become. He doesn't know what I've lost. And he has no idea what I'm willing to do now.*

He's shown to a seat equipped with gleaming holographic touchpads. As he sits, the table comes to life. Projections dancing in the air above it. Mallory keeps his posture composed, but his eyes scan the room.

These men shaped the modern world from behind closed doors. And now they're pretending to include me. They still think I'm just a tool. A weapon they can point and forget. But they don't know what I've seen. What I've lost. I'm not here to play by their rules anymore.

Trent's smile sharpens, as if to say: "You listen to me. I hold the reins."

"Mr. Vice President, thank you for coming on such short notice," Trent says.

"We were hoping to say *President* Mallory by now," Sir Peter Murton adds with calm precision.

"As was I," Mallory replies coolly, glancing toward the English peer. "The President's health is my most pressing concern."

Jean Rousseaux leans forward. In his throaty French accent, he asks, "We are given to understand he is paralyzed?"

"Yes, but still able to function," Mallory cuts in sharply.

"Touché," Rousseaux mutters.

The German industrialist taps his touchpad. A holographic *Time Magazine* cover appears above the table, featuring a striking woman in her mid-forties with intense eyes and a calm, enigmatic smile. The headline reads: The Woman Who Rewired Reality.

"Dr. Jessica Peake," Trent says. "The reason we're here, gentlemen."

The image fades, replaced by a map of Asia. It zooms in on what used to be a remote village in Afghanistan that's now barren earth.

"Ab Barik," Mallory says. "Not what I expected."

"And not what we expected," the German replies. "An entire village gone. Without a trace."

The image enlarges, revealing scorched earth. An eerie absence of life.

"Is she responsible for this? If not her, then who?" the German demands. "We've lost an entire facility. Dozens of personnel unaccounted for. Military, too. And the last person to sign off, if memory serves, was Dr. Peake. She was told not to proceed until she notified us about further developments in her neutrino research."

Rain slashes against the windows. The room falls silent.

Dr. Liu Wen speaks from a corner of the table. "Her final transmission warned us of a systems breach that should not have been overlooked by us.

"At the moment, it's being treated as a NATO issue," he adds. "Like ANITA in Antarctica. And Russia now has its Neutrino Ice Towers on the East Coast, stored in containment vats."

Mallory gives a thin smile. "Comparing those to Jessica Peake's work is like comparing apples to hand grenades."

He remains still, gaze sweeping the table.

"We must also not forget," he says, "That Peake was operating under direct Consortium oversight. If she failed, *We* failed."

"When Washington cut her funding," Trent interjects, "*we* stepped in. In return, she promised exclusivity and a technology that would neutralize every weapons platform in the world."

Trent pushes his chair back, attempting to stand.

"You still have it," Mallory says.

"Not if it isn't working," Murton snaps, lighting another cigarette. He inhales and exhales. "And it clearly isn't."

The Japanese Yakuza figure, silent until now, speaks with quiet menace. "Meanwhile, Dr. Peake lives in a compound on an island paradise that we paid for."

"Her patents paid for it," Mallory counters. "She's independently wealthy. That makes her harder to control. And I hope you understand that she is a protagonist, a scientist whose inventions blur the line between science and a miracle."

Sir Peter Murton stands, voice tight. "But control is what you promised! And you've apparently lost it."

Trent taps another command. A glowing globe appears above the table, showing a world reshaped: The Union of Federated Soviet Territories, a fractured Africa, the People's Republic of Chinese Asia, a rising India. Red dots pulse across the map.

"Nine G-22 nations have fallen to extremists," Trent says.

"And thanks to Turkey going fully nuclear, after years of regional instability and her shifting alliances," Murton adds, "the Middle East is a tinderbox. We now have ten."

The globe flattens into a map, instability highlighted across regions.

"The Union of Federated Soviet Territories has become a toy store for terrorists," the Russian adds. "Their arms limitation treaty with the U.S is a running joke."

The Yakuza speaks again through the hologram. "One that Chinese Asia doesn't find amusing. In fact, they're ramping up their nukes as fast as they can make them."

Mallory leans back. "None of them have what we have."

"But we don't have it," Murton says, stubbing out his cigarette. "And we don't have *her.*"

He opens his cigarette case again.

"I have her," Mallory says coldly, pausing. "I hold her contract."

"Then see to it she makes good on it," Trent says. "Or we'll be forced to terminate it. This meeting is over. Mr. Vice President, finish what you began! Then we can talk again. And make certain that Dr. Jessica Peake knows who is actually funding her and more importantly that it's *our* weapon."

He rises with the help of an aide and walks slowly from the room.

Mallory stands silently, eyes sweeping the table. He nods once to the English peer, then to the French financier. Without a word, he turns and exits.

A deafening crack of thunder shakes the mansion as lightning splits the sky. Mallory walks quickly from the room, the storm at his back.

SEVEN

Echoes across empires

FROM FAR ABOVE THE EARTH, the world seems deceptively tranquil. A satellite glides silently over Southeast Asia, its gaze tracing the once-familiar contours of Thailand's ornate temples, now blended into a greater whole. The heavens continue their silent journey northward, sweeping across the vast stretches of Myanmar and Mongolia, until they reach the shimmering heart of a new empire: Beijing.

As dusk settles over the People's Republic of Chinese Asia, the city's skyline unfolds like a digital tapestry. Gleaming towers rise in perfect symmetry, their glass and steel facades catching the last golden rays of sunlight. At the center of it all, nestled atop the majestic Jade Spring Hill Palace, the ancient and the ultramodern converge in a harmony of power and prestige.

Once a symbol of imperial legacy, the palace has been transformed into a sprawling private residence. Military convoys circle its mountainous perimeter. A blend of civilian and state security forces stands vigil. Inside, opulence reigns, silk, jade, and lacquered wood adorn every surface.

On the third floor, in a room draped in deep red silk, Chinese Premier Yang Bin Rong sits at his desk. In his early fifties, he appears youthful, though the weight of responsibility has etched itself into his posture. His reading glasses rest beside a classified report, boldly stamped:

TOP SECRET: THE AB BARIK INCIDENT

He reads it again, slower this time, then picks up the phone and dials.

"Mr. Chairman," comes the voice of Hui Chen, head of the Ministry of State Security, China's formidable intelligence agency.

"I just read the brief on Ab Barik," Yang says, his voice calm but clipped. "I find it utterly inadequate."

"As did I, Mr. Chairman," Hui replies. "Then again, the event is only a few hours old."

Yang rises and steps out into the rooftop garden. Below him, the lights of Beijing glitter like stars trapped beneath glass. He breathes in the cool night air, the weight of global uncertainty pressing against his chest.

"Apparently, hours wasted," he mutters. "Do we have a technology that overlaps this or not?"

There's a pause. Hui's voice returns, cautious. "Uncertain as of yet. I understand that we are close."

"You are head of the Guoanbu and my Intelligence Chief," Yang snaps. "For that, I require certainty. I need a full report within forty-eight hours."

"Shì. Lìjí. You shall have it, sir."

They hang up in unison. Yang turns and motions for his assistant.

Moscow

Dawn breaks, and snow dusts the streets and rooftops of the Kremlin. The city's storefronts glitter with international brands and post-Soviet ambition. Superimposed against the rising sun, the spires of the Kremlin cast long shadows over the capital of the *Union of Federated Soviet Territories.*

Inside the New Kremlin, President Alexi Karpov sits in a worn leather chair by a roaring fireplace. Rugged and composed, he wears power like a second skin. Two women, barely clothed, lie tangled in the firelight. He doesn't look at them, his eyes are fixed on the iPad in his hand.

A top aide approaches, handing him a secure summary of the Ab Barik incident.

"Everything? Everyone?" Karpov asks.

The aide nods silently. "They're going to blame us for this, you know."

"Not this time, I think." Karpov stands, snapping his fingers. The women scramble to gather their belongings and vanish without a word. His aide pours him a vodka.

"Good," Karpov says, accepting the glass. "Then break this down for me from the beginning."

Washington D.C.

The White House stands bathed in morning light. Inside the Situation Room, the walls are alive with news. Four major networks—ABC, CNN, MSNBC, and BBC—broadcast simultaneously, each relaying the same chilling story from the Hindu Kush mountains of Afghanistan.

The ABC Anchor reports: *"One of the most bizarre and terrifying events in decades took place yesterday when the entire mountain village of Ab Barik completely disappeared…"*

BBC (on-site) says: *"Even more ironic are eyewitness reports that a firefight was underway between NATO Army Rangers and Islamic State Rebels when the mysterious disintegration occurred…"*

CNN reports: *"Thus far, all major powers have denied either knowledge or responsibility for this mind-boggling event. All attempts to identify the source of this so-called 'death ray' have failed. Zero results."*

In the inner chamber of a spacious two-room suite in the White House, President Walter Hamilton mutes the multi-screen broadcasts flickering before him. Three phones sit beside his bed: one red, one blue, one black. Fully dressed, two nurses help him carefully into a wheelchair. His legs, weakened from a month of immobility, have already begun to atrophy.

The red phone begins to ring. Hamilton turns, about to answer it, as Chief of Staff Nicholas Porter enters. The phone continues to ring.

"I have it, sir," Porter says, stepping forward and answering the red line with practiced calm. "Alpha Lion 1. Yes, of course." He hands the receiver to Hamilton. "Premier Yang, sir. Wishing to speak with you."

Porter rolls a small side table in front of the President and places the phone carefully on it.

Hamilton nods to the nurse and aide. "Oh—and Porter, please turn on the overhead screen for me and Premier Yang. Thank you."

Without hesitation, Porter touches the correct switch, closing the door behind him as he exits.

"Hello, Premier Yang," Hamilton says, his voice steady but strained. "Where are you?"

"In Beijing," Yang replies. His voice is loud and clear as his image appears on the screens before Hamilton. He sits behind a massive desk, the skyline glowing behind him as the sun dips low.

"Wishing you a speedy recovery, of course, Mr. President," he says. "Ordinarily, I would not disturb you at such a time. However…"

He pauses, waiting to see if Hamilton will finish the thought. Hamilton flinches, pain flaring in his side. "Yes, the Afghani village—Ab Barik, I believe. It wasn't us. And it wasn't NATO."

"You, Mr. President, are NATO," Yang replies. "And our latest intel informs us it wasn't Russia either. It's too sophisticated to be one of the rogue nuclear nations. But it did take place just outside the Central Asian Plague Band, where Islamic State rebels now control everything. Something like this could spread the contagion again—like a firestorm."

"Or shut it down for good," Hamilton offers.

Yang pauses. "Well, that would be quite some technology if it did. Do you know something we do not?"

"We're not entirely sure," Hamilton admits. "I have my team on it."

"And I have mine," Yang says. "They never fail."

"Then we'll get to the bottom of this. Find out who and why. Sooner rather than later."

Hamilton's resolve is clear, though fatigue creeps into his voice. Yang notices.

"I think that's essential, Mr. President. And I wish you continued success in your recovery from the assassination attempt."

As the call ends, Hamilton exhales slowly, deeply. Porter, clearly aware the conversation has concluded, enters the room, shuts down the screen, removes the table, and replaces the red phone.

"He knows," the President says quietly. "He knows a great deal. The question is, do we?"

Porter doesn't hesitate. "It's got to be Jessica Peake."

"That much is a given," Hamilton replies. "At this point, she's in the crosshairs of a dozen interested parties. So, at this point, I need my Number Two."

EIGHT

The weight of morning

THE HOUSE STANDS WITH the quiet dignity of age, perched among the trees like a relic that has outlived its time. One Observatory Circle, official residence of the Vice President of the United States—wakes slowly, its bones creaking in the hush of early light. The air is still, as if even the wind respects the secrets that live here.

Inside, Douglas Mallory sleeps soundly, the weight of power momentarily forgotten beneath the warmth of tangled sheets and bare skin. His breath is steady, his body curled around another. Digby Stahl lies beside him, silent, his back turned. His presence is more than just a lover's comfort, he is a cipher, a confidant, a man who knows how to disappear when needed.

Then comes the sound.

A sharp vibration sudden and insistent. The second of two phones, always the second, buzzes against the nightstand like a warning shot. Mallory's eyes snap open. Gone is the softness of sleep. The mask returns in an instant.

He sits bolt upright, voice cool and composed. "Mr. President, good morning. Glad you're back in the mix."

The words come easily, but his mind is already racing. He rubs at his eyes, the dream world receding. Digby stirs but doesn't speak.

Mallory shakes his head, trying to loosen his stiff neck, coming fully awake.

"Yes, I'm aware. I've been brought totally up to speed. Fourteen hundred hours. Of course, I'll be right there."

He ends the call and sits for a moment, the silence pressing in again. The gravity of the day begins to shift in his chest.

"Well now…" he murmurs, more to himself than to anyone else.

He swings his legs over the side of the bed and slaps Digby playfully on the rear. "Get dressed, Digby. We've got places to be."

The White House is always colder than it looks. Beneath the grandeur and gilded edges, it is a place of calculation, of haunted history, and political ghosts. Mallory ascends the grand staircase, the red carpet soft beneath his polished shoes. Two Secret Service agents follow at a respectful distance.

One of them, Digby, again wears the uniform of the day: dark suit, smart glasses, expression unreadable. The night's intimacy is gone, replaced by the rigid choreography of protocol.

Mallory doesn't look back. He doesn't need to.

President Hamilton waits in the office suite, seated in a wheelchair that seems both foreign and final. The man who once commanded rooms with a glance now wears a Navy cardigan embroidered with the Presidential Seal. His face is thinner, his hair streaked with gray, but his eyes still hold the sharpness of a man who has not yet surrendered.

Porter stands behind him, arms crossed. Two nurses exit quietly as Mallory enters.

"Doug Mallory," the President says with a weary smile. "Fit and rested. I've asked Nick Porter to sit in."

"Of course," Mallory replies, nodding to Porter, who offers a curt acknowledgment.

Porter waves the nurses away. The room grows heavier.

"Mr. Vice President, you've been a traveling man," Porter says, his voice cool.

"Big shoes to fill," Mallory replies, taking a step toward him.

Hamilton leans forward slightly. His voice drops. "I'm afraid you're going to have to fill them sooner than you think, Doug. That's part of the reason I called you in. To confirm what the world will soon know—I'm officially paraplegic." He gestures toward the chair. "This is my new reality."

Mallory's expression remains composed, but inside, something tightens. The finality of it is undeniable. Hamilton gestures for him to sit down. As he takes his seat, he says quietly, "It was the same for FDR, sir. And he did pretty well in his time."

"Different time. Different era. This is degenerative. The shooter's bullet did its job. I'll hold on for a year at best. Then, in my last year, you'll step in. That will give you the unassailable advantage of incumbency."

Mallory's mind is already calculating the implications. Timing. Optics. Momentum.

"How many people know about your decision?"

"For now? Just the three of us." Hamilton's gaze shifts to the window. "Tomorrow's a different story. But today, we have a more pressing issue."

"Jessica Peake," Mallory says. "Your creature."

"My friend," Hamilton corrects. "Not quite the test run we'd discussed."

"We didn't discuss it," Mallory replies. "And *we* didn't order it, even though our NATO partners think we did. Congress defunded her two years ago. That gives you plausible deniability."

Hamilton arches an eyebrow, bites his lip. "But you went to your dark money sources to subsidize her, didn't you?" He shakes his head.

Mallory meets his gaze without flinching. "No strings. At your request."

Hamilton sighs. "At this point, I have amnesia. And at this point, I need you to get to her under the radar. I trust you still have a relationship with her."

Mallory gives a faint smile. "Let's just say we understand each other."

"Sometimes, that's all you need. Let's move on this yesterday. The U.S. is still going to get tagged with this unless we can get an exculpatory declaration from her."

Mallory stands and walks to the President, lowering his head slightly. "We know where she lives. And where she keeps her hillside labs, sir."

The morning sun has climbed higher now, casting long shadows across the marble floors. Mallory descends the staircase outside the Presidential Office, his pace brisk, his mind focused.

Digby follows, once again in step behind him, joined by another agent. The rhythm of the day has begun.

Mallory allows himself a small grin. "I love it when things work out."

But even as he says it, he knows nothing ever really works out … *Not in this town. Not for long.*

NINE

The shape of shadows

THE CORRIDORS OF THE KREMLIN lie cold and silent, like the breath of a sleeping giant. Shadows stretch long across the polished marble, broken only by the clipped footsteps of Defense Minister Ivgeny Maxim and the woman beside him, Captain Kamila Dimitriova. She carries a thick folder tucked under one arm, a data disk in the other. Her expression is undecipherable, hidden behind the practiced veil of military composure.

They pass beneath the gilded archway into the UFST Council Chamber a vaulted room where power hums through the air like static. Waiting inside, Alexandre Karpov stands with arms folded, his eyes sharp beneath the weight of a sleepless night. Beside him looms General Vasily Kalischenko, a man carved from stone, his medals glinting like old wounds.

"Maxim," Karpov says, voice low, expectant. "You always come through. What have you found? How do we deal with this? And where," he leans in slightly, "do the breadcrumbs lead?"

Maxim offers a slight nod. His voice is steady, grave. "All imprints point to an American particle physicist, Dr. Jessica Peake." He pauses, letting the name settle like dust across the table. "*Time Magazine's* Person of the Year, 2029. Graduated summa cum laude from Harvard. Ph.D. from MIT. Quantum physics. Specializes in high-energy particle dissemination using Neutrinos."

Karpov arches a brow. "Sounds expensive. Any chance we can buy her?"

"Unlikely," Maxim replies. "She's a patriot. And a rich one. But eccentric. Once made an entire concert shell in New York vanish into thin air."

He gestures to Dimitriova, who steps forward. Her fingers dance across the control pad. A hologram flickers to life above the table. A woman's face emerges, tall, lean, and striking. Aquiline features, with the poise of someone who stopped doubting herself long ago.

"At forty-one," Dimitriova begins, her voice cool and precise, "she is worth approximately one hundred and thirty-one million U.S. dollars. Mostly acquired from patents."

The hologram shifts, showing schematics, prototypes, blueprints, and a retractable, invisible face mask—devices that look like they belong to another century, one that hasn't happened yet.

"She is brilliant," Dimitriova continues. "So, the short answer to your question is no, probably not. Her research, however, requires deep pockets. In 2029, Congress granted her $1.5 billion. Then without explanation, they pulled the plug."

Karpov narrows his eyes. "So, all evidence from Ab Barik leads back to Dr. Peake's neutrino experiments?"

Maxim nods. "She was testing something. Something… off the books."

Karpov's lips curl into a thin smile. "Neutrinos. She sounds utterly unpredictable. That means we can get to her."

Maxim hesitates. "That might prove difficult."

"Difficult," Dimitriova cuts in, her voice like a blade unsheathed, "but not impossible."

The chamber dims. The hologram shifts again, this time, to a place far from the Kremlin's cold marble and steel.

"This is where she hides out." Dimitriova says. "The Caribbean. St. George, American Virgin Islands." Her voice seems to echo through the room.

From high above, the villa unfolds like a dream etched into the cliffside. Three sweeping wings jut toward the sea, encased in glass and solar paneling, framed by a living roof of wild grass, it is a fortress of elegance, zero-energy efficient, self-sustaining, and heavily guarded.

"She lives alone," Dimitriova says softly, the images flickering around them. "Thirty hectares. A converted British fort. The grounds are protected by a 210-degree scan system—land and sea. Laser scanners. Motion sensors. A private runway with a Learjet. A heliport."

The camera sweeps lower. The perimeter wall rises—thick, unyielding. Below, the ocean roars against the rocks like a warning.

"She built this place to vanish," she adds. "And she has the means to disappear, should she choose to."

Karpov stares at the face of Jessica Peake, frozen mid-blink in the hologram. Her expression is unreadable.

"Then we must find her… before she chooses to vanish again."

And in the silence that follows, the room tilts toward shadow, toward the edge of something vast. Something unknowable. Something that shimmers just beyond the reach of reason.

TEN

The weight of light

THE SKY BLEEDS A PALE gold over the sea. Slightly in need of a wash- job, a red Jeep Wrangler pulls up to the main gate and slows just enough for it to swing open. Inside John Taylor, a thirty something IT genius and tech nerd, thumbs up the Security Team who wave him through.

He speeds up the tree lined driveway and crunches to a halt outside the villa. The sun hangs low, a molten coin on the horizon, casting long shadows that stretch like fingers across the gravel. He kills the engine and sits for a moment, hands resting on the wheel, listening to the tick of the cooling engine and the distant cry of gulls. Then without hesitation dashes up the steps into the Villa.

Inside, the house is quiet too quiet. It is a long elegant hallway peppered with abstract paintings, granite floors and a long antique Persian runner.

At the end Maggie a thickset very British personal assistant meets him. Her expression unreadable, her arms folded tightly across her chest. She doesn't speak. She simply nods and nods toward a circular glassed-in lift.

"In the tower," she says and points above her.

Taylor turns and asks as he walks past her, "How is she?"

"How do you think, John?"

Taylor exhales through his nose, then steps inside the glass elevator. As it rises, the ocean unfurls around him like a living mural, blue-gray and endless, a mirror to the chaos below.

The doors whisper open to the Tower.

The tower bedroom and den have a one-hundred-and-eighty-degree view of the ocean and surrounding islands. Jessica Peake is curled on the floor, her back against the wall, knees drawn up to her chest. Her face is pale, lips cracked, eyes rimmed red from tears and sleepless nights. The bottle of Black Cow vodka, a hollowed-out relic of her spiral, hangs from her hand. Clearly intoxicated, she hears Taylor kneel beside her, careful not to startle her. She tries to take another swig.

"Jess?" he says softly.

Jessica her voice raspy. "Johnny, my boy, come join me for a martini. Not shaken, not stirred. No olive. Just the straight shit, just as Ian Fleming would have wanted."

The bottle slips from her hand. "I can't stop seeing him, Johnny. The boy. His eyes. Like he was staring straight through me."

Taylor places a hand on her shoulder. "Drinking in the middle of the day? We're going to fix this."

Jessica lets out a bitter laugh. "Well, why not? It isn't every day you get to have a Black Cow with a mass murderer. You think this can be fixed? You think we can just *undo* a supernova?"

"No! You're not a mass murderer," he admits.

"Oh yeah?! Then what am I?"

"No," he says. "They may just be displaced. We can understand it. We can learn from it. And maybe...just maybe...we can stop it from happening again."

Noting the irony, Jessica laughs and begins to cry at the same time.

She turns to face him now, her expression raw. "*Displaced?* God, John, be my PR guru! *Where exactly were they displaced to? Valhalla?* I didn't just miscalculate. I ignored the signs. I was so *sure*. So goddamn sure."

Taylor helps her to her feet. She sways, but he steadies her. Tapping his iPhone, he shouts, "Maggie! Coffee! Atlantis. Now."

He walks Jessica slowly out of the room. "Let's go and see what we can do."

The control center hums like a living organism. Jessica calls her war room *Atlantis*. Screens flicker with cascading data, star maps, energy readouts. The ceiling above them ripples with the refracted light of the glass bottom of the swimming pool, casting waves across Jessica's face as she takes her seat at the primary console.

There is another glass wall that faces her as she sits at her console. It reveals a connection to a crystal-clear underwater cave where a community of ocean creatures from clownfish and groupers to barracuda, even a sea turtle come and go within the clear waters.

A large OLED screen mounted on a central wall above a multi-image holographic workstation displays the frozen, dust-covered face of the young petrified boy as he runs toward his injured mother…a look of horror mars his face.

"What have I done, John?! Oh God! *What have I done?* She sits motionless in front of several thin, transparent keyboards and screens. She is haunted by the frozen image of the boy with his mother lying face down in the mountain stream.

"I'm a terminal fuck-up! I totally misjudged…" she says turning away from the console.

"You didn't. There's been an overload in the Neutrino Dome." He points to the screen directly in front of him.

Jessica is shocked, in disbelief. "No way! It can't be! Did you cross check energy levels in the oscillator before we shot?

"Yes, but now it shows an overload." Taylor calls up the results on one of the screens.

Jessica reads from the screen, "What was the influence level in the Neutrino Propagator?"

"The output was just above ten to the fifteenth Joules." Taylor refreshes the information on the screen.

Focusing on the information before her, Jessica presses several commands into a keyboard and the screen goes black for a second before an image of the central region of our galaxy appears.

Jessica stands and looks closer at the screen. "Okay, I remember now. Months ago…that unusual glow from that star in our galaxy."

Taylor remembers, "Yeah but that star wasn't from our galaxy. We found it in Andromeda." He slides his chair to another console, already typing. He enters several commands, and the image on the screen rapidly changes along with the tracking digits.

The image begins to slow down as it arrives at the outer edge of the NGC-752 galaxy. A glow emanates from its left wing.

Jessica, enthused says, "You are so right. So right. I remember now, Andromeda the Virgo cluster! It was the star named after that hockey player."

"You mean Mark Messier? What a mnemonic…Messier 91."

"Bring up the data from the last pulse," Jessica orders, her voice steadier now, clipped and precise. "I want to see the propagation pattern." She continues to nervously rock back and forth in her swivel chair.

He looks at her and complies. The central screen blossoms with a burst of red and violet, an expanding shockwave, beautiful and terrible.

"There," she whispers. "Messier 91. That's where it started. I should never have dismissed it. I am so dumb."

Taylor frowns. "But we weren't targeting anything in that region. That's over sixty million light-years away."

Jessica's fingers fly across the interface. "I know. But the resonance signature matches. The neutrino spike, the gamma burst, it's all there."

On the screen the red gas cloud glows with ever-changing light, Illuminated by an expanding shock wave—the aftermath of a Supernova.

"Look at me. I'm a bloody nervous wreck! The bloody day I decide to go ahead, we get hit with the after effects of a massive Supernova. Maybe thirteen trillion kilometers across. So, I have to wonder…Who or what is on my side?"

A silence falls between them, heavy with implication.

"You're saying we triggered it?" he asks.

"I'm saying…" She hesitates, then breathes out. "I'm saying we might have amplified something that was already unstable. Like a whisper in the right frequency that shatters glass."

Taylor leans back, stunned. "Jesus."

She walks away from her console to the glass wall and smashes her hand in frustration on the glass. Taylor comes over to join her. Her meltdown finished, she rights herself with military bearing, walks back to the workstation area.

She sits down, then abruptly stands and starts pacing. "This changes everything. The Principle, it's not just about observation. It's influence. Interaction. We're not just watching the universe anymore, John. We're touching it."

He runs a hand through his hair. "And it's touching back."

Jessica leans into the screen as Taylor pours himself another coffee.

He takes a drink, then spits it out. "God, this is the worst coffee I've ever had in my life. Shit, Maggie!"

"Part of our atonement is we have bad coffee down here," Jessica says. "Upstairs is better."

"No sin can be this great."

"Maggie has other talents." Jessica's eyes meet his, fierce now. "We need to recalibrate the entire system. Strip it down to the base code. If we're going to keep using the Irenic Interface, we need to understand its reach."

Taylor nods. "I'll go back to the Dome, start dumping the core data." He begins to leave.

"Good," she says, calls to him. "And John?"

He pauses at the door.

"Thank you," she says quietly. "For not giving up on me."

He offers a small smile. "You'd do the same."

Jessica turns back to the screen, the red glow of Messier 91 still pulsing like a wound across the stars. Her reflection stares back at her, haunted, resolute.

As John walks away from her, she realizes that for her he definitely was the right choice. She talks to herself as she observes various images from the village disappearance that she pulls up on a screen. *His demeanor is calm and deliberate, reflecting a deep commitment to peaceful resolution and mutual understanding. Rather than reacting emotionally or taking sides, John emphasizes dialogue and empathy with our work and often he will encourage others to consider perspectives beyond their own.*

The universe has spoken. And she is listening now. John marks a subtle turning point in her character. Up to that moment, she's been skeptical, sharp, even confrontational, but this quiet observation reveals that she sees something admirable in his approach.

This moment of introspection from Jessica suggests she's beginning to reconsider her own methods, or at least open herself to a broader view.

She walks toward the glass ocean wall, observing the grace of various fish and reflects on herself, her actions and now her guilt. "I need a drink!" she says, smiling at the small turtle whose face is nuzzled up to the glass. "Can I get you one?"

ELEVEN

Shadows and still water

IN A PRIVATE KREMLIN OFFICE, sunlight filters through heavy drapes, casting long shadows across a polished table. Karpov sits across from Maxim and Dimitriova, pen in hand, eyes sharp with intent.

Karpov's voice is quiet, calculated—a whisper that cuts through the silence like a scalpel. "We need the technology Jessica Peake possesses by any means necessary. So how do we get to her?"

"The old-fashioned way," Maxim says, his voice devoid of irony. "Abduction. Persuasion. Conversion."

Karpov leans in. "Where is she vulnerable? Does she have a family?"

Dimitriova's answer is a slow, deliberate contradiction. "Yes and no." There is an obvious long silence and Dimitriova uses the silence to exit.

Jessica Peake's Villa

It's noon in the Caribbean and the suns heat has yet to break through the shade of the tall tropical palms. The gates of the villa swing open for a metallic blue Mini Cooper, its convertible top catching the light like a sapphire. The guards wave it through—familiar faces, trusted ones.

The car rolls to a stop in the circular drive. Mark Richards steps out, tall, confident, effortlessly handsome. He lowers a tiny tricycle to the ground, his six-year-old daughter, Lori, squealing with delight as she climbs aboard. Her handlebar basket overflows with super-toys.

Maggie greets Mark with a warm hug. Lori takes off like a shot, pedaling furiously toward the infinity pool, weaving between palm trees with fearless joy. But then a miscalculation. One back wheel slips over the edge.

The tricycle, the toys, and Lori tumble into the water.

"Lori, no!" Mark shouts, his voice cracking. "Oh Jesus, Lori!" Without hesitation, he dives in.

Below, in the hidden sanctum of the villa, Jessica's lab, her Atlantis, screens flicker with Neutrino count values. She cross checks them, shifting particle maps. She's deep in focus, lost in the dance of data, until…Movement in the water above.

Through the transparent ceiling, Jessica sees Lori sinking, still clinging to the tricycle. Mark is just behind her, arms outstretched.

Jessica bolts upright. "Hold on! I'm on my way!"

She rips away from the console, bypasses the elevator, flies up the narrow stairwell, skipping steps, urgency in every breath.

Maggie kneels by the pool, towel in hand. Mark surfaces, gasping, and lifts Lori onto the deck. Jessica rushes in, soaked in adrenaline.

"Mark, I'm so sorry! Are you two okay?"

Mark doesn't answer. He's too focused on Lori, who bursts into tears.

"Daddy! My Super Girl! My friends! They'll drown!"

Without a word, Jessica dives in. Moments later, she surfaces, triumphant, clutching all three toys. She hands them to Lori, who hugs Super Girl tightly to her.

"You're cool, Jess," the little girl says, beaming.

Jessica laughs, breathless. "Glad somebody thinks so."

Mark toweling himself dry. "Forgot we were coming, didn't you?"

Jessica turns to Maggie. "Could you get Lori inside? Dry clothes guest room, maybe?"

"By all means," Maggie says. "We'll go in and have a nice cup of tea, won't we, Lori?"

"Hot chocolate," Lori corrects.

"Hot chocolate it is." Maggie responds.

As they disappear into the villa, Jessica wraps a towel around her waist, peeling off drenched shorts. She wipes water from her eyes and pushes her wet hair from her forehead while Maggie finishes drying Lori.

Mark watches her with a wry smile. "Never a dull moment."

"She could've drowned," Jessica mutters. "God, I should've been up here."

Mark pulls off his drenched shirt, wrings it out, and dries off slowly. "You know I don't mind being an afterthought. But Lori might start to take it personally."

"You're not an afterthought," she says, stepping closer. "You're sanctuary. You two are my only sane points of reference."

She kisses him deeply, fully. Their shared wetness and warmth steams off their skin. Emphasizes their sensuality.

"If this is appeasement," Mark says, "it's working."

Jessica grins "Then let me work on you further." Both her hands grab his butt and press him against her. He glances around. "It will be time for Lori's nap is in an hour or two."

"Sweet little girl," Jessica murmurs. "Needs her rest."

Later, in the guest bedroom, Lori sleeps soundly beneath soft covers. Maggie walks quietly to the door and touches a switch, the high-tech sunshades close and she tiptoes out.

Jessica and Mark, post coital, lay bathed in the dusk gold and violet light that bounces from the reflection of the sun on the ocean. They lie tangled in each other, half-covered by soft Egyptian linen and dreams.

"You're staying the night, right?" she murmurs.

"I hope to hell," he replies. "It's a ferry ride back. Might as well be a day trip."

Jessica sighs. "I wish you could be here always. You and Lori."

"You know the deal," Mark says.

"I do," she says. "But it doesn't make it easier."

He turns to her. "Your work... which you never discuss. Damn, but you're a living contradiction."

"It's dicey," she says. "And it's dangerous."

"You work at a computer console all day. How dangerous can that be?"

"You have no idea."

Mark added, almost in a whisper, "You know, I shouldn't have to remind you that we're practically in the same field. I've got degrees in biomedical engineering and quantum physics." He said, half smiling. "Do those count for anything?"

Jessica didn't answer. She held his gaze, then turned to pour a glass of water. The sound of it filling the glass broke the silence.

Mark pulled the top sheet off her to uncover her beautiful, sculptured, Rodinesque butt.

She turned, slapped his hand and said, "You like that, don't you? Later." She placed the glass down, got out of bed and crossed to the window. The fabric of her slip caught the soft light as the moon turned the sea to silver over black.

As Mark got out of bed to join her, Jessica turned. "They count for a great deal, Mark." She turned back to look out at the ocean as it began to rain.

Mark joined her and wrapped his arms around her waist. "The line between focus and obsession is a very thin one. Have you crossed it?" He whispered as he kissed her neck.

"I'm not sure it matters," she said. "Only the endgame matters."

Mark smiled faintly. "And therein lies the conundrum of Jessica Peake."

She responded by biting her lip, removing his hands, crossing the room and slipping into a robe. "But this is at a different level."

He nodded. "The Nobel nominee in Neutrino Capture and Particle Physics. Have they weaponized you yet?"

Jessica smirked. "Loaded question. Dinner?"

At the dining table, laughter filled the room. Burgers, fries, and chicken were passed around. Jessica dangled a fry towards Mark, who snapped at it playfully.

"Oh look, Mark bit my finger off!" she gasped.

"No!" Lori giggled. "He didn't!"

"He drew blood!"

"It's ketchup!"

Jessica tucked back an index finger so only the knuckle showed. "I'm missing one. See?"

Mark pulled a fry from his mouth. "Here it is. And I'm going to eat it!"

He chomped the fry. Jessica screamed. Lori screamed louder, laughing.

Jessica revealed her finger. "Fake! Here's the real one!"

Lori hugged her tight. Jessica gazed across the table at Mark.

"Oh... more like this," she whispered. Mark reached for her hand. "We're right here."

Night settled in. Jessica and Mark lay together, arms entwined. Sleepy-eyed and clutching her toy, Lori climbed into bed beside them. Mark gently released his hold on Jessica to cradle Lori, drawing her close. They watched her eyes flutter shut.

Mark's voice was low, shaped more in his chest than his throat. "When Nancy died I came apart. Like the ground I was standing on just didn't exist anymore. But Lori." He stopped, jaw tight. "She pulled me back. The trust in her eyes makes me stand taller. Reminds me who I should be. She's my anchor."

"She's changed you," Jessica said quietly. "And she is why I continue to do what I continue to do. For her, and for all the children who'll grow up with her. That's what keeps me steady."

Later still, the room was quiet. Jessica, Mark, and Lori slept in a tangle of limbs and warmth. Carefully, Jessica eased out of bed. She slipped into jeans and a shirt, then gently lifted Supergirl from Lori's loose grip. She stepped out into the night, leaving the comfort of love behind, drawn once more to the shadows of her work and the storm it might yet bring.

TWELVE

The edge beyond knowing

JESSICA SITS ALONE in the glow of her command center. Three screens, three truths, three windows into the impossible. She runs an algorithm on them.

On the first screen, the Messier 91 galaxy unfurls like a cosmic wound. A supernova pulses at its center, its galactic arms spinning outward in a silent ballet of destruction and rebirth.

The second screen is chaos incarnate: a storm of neutrinos, shifting, colliding, dissolving. They form, reform, and scatter in bursts of invisible energy particles without mass, without anchor, threading the universe with indifference. They form in clusters, it seems, in explosions of undirected energy. Until now. Until she gives them purpose. Until she gives them charge.

The third screen is the most human and the most unbearable. Faces emerge in a montage from the Ab Barik incident: soldiers, rebels, villagers, a terrified three-year-old boy. Still frames, frozen in the moment before erasure. A village gone. A memory displaced. A consequence unfolding. One by one, she views them, then immediately changes the frame to view yet another horror.

Jessica's fingers move across three keyboards in a rhythm only she understands. Each keystroke alters the next. Each variable redefines the last. The neutrinos affect the images. The images shift the equations. The equations bend the stars.

"What created that vast empowered light that embraced and dissolved everything within its radiance?" Jessica wonders out loud in the empty chamber. Her sanctuary.

She almost seemed frantic, working from the three screens simultaneously now. First the neutrinos as they disintegrated human cells, to the Ab Barik images of the villagers as they disappeared, moving calculations until the first invariably changes the nature of the others that followed.

Behind her, the elevator opens with a soft sigh. Mark steps into the room. He stops, stunned. His breath catches in his throat.

"God," he says. "You're that guy." He points to the screens. "Did you do that?"

Jessica turns to face him, but she doesn't retreat. She doesn't soften. She doesn't defuse what he's just seen. "Mark," she says. "You truly have no idea."

"I know supernovas when I see them." He replies, stepping closer. "I know neutrino clusters when I see them. You're not the only one out here pushing the edge."

"This is a whole new edge," she says. "Beyond anything anyone's ever done."

"You know, that's what they said with the Manhattan Project." He pauses, his voice darkening. "Obviously you're trying to recalibrate the eradication of the Afghani village. Was it you? Are you the mysterious cause?"

"Mark." Her voice is firm. "It's on a need-to-know basis. And at this point… you do not need to know."

She, at this point, has not taken her gaze away from the horror on the screens.

"Who were they? Do you even know? Do you even give a shit?" His voice rises. "You're so cryptic I need a decoder just to have a conversation."

Jessica turns to face Mark. As she does so, she freezes the screens. "You told me you would never interfere with my work or question me on it," she says. "And yet here you are way, way, *way* out of your depth."

"I know enough to know your research is dangerous," Mark says. "Neutrino research is the great unknown quantity."

"They permeate everything," Jessica says. "They pass through everything and everyone by the billions every nanosecond."

"Without electrical charge," he interrupts. "Therefore, they interrupt nothing. Unless you give them a charge. Unless you force them into a behavior they weren't designed for. Is that what you've done?"

"You have no idea what we've done," she says. "We only wanted to eliminate the weapons." She holds her fingers out, showing the sliver of space between them. "We were that close."

Mark grabs his head, as if the truth is physically painful. "Jesus," he mutters. "Listen to yourself. I wonder if that's what they said at Nagasaki or Chernobyl. You're playing with human lives. And what you've apparently found is just a cleaner way to kill."

Jessica's eyes flash. "You stupid, arrogant shit!" she says. "You're living testimony to the fact that a little knowledge is a dangerous thing. We've found a way to transcend life. We can move matter. Move it."

She gestures to the Super Girl toy at the edge of her console. With a few keystrokes, it vanishes. Then, another a second later, it reappears at the corner where Mark is standing.

He seems gob smacked. He stares at it, speechless.

"You have no idea what we can do," she says.

"Toys," Mark says. "You're playing with toys that you somehow conflate with reality. Jesus, lady. This is something you can't control. And you can't, can you? That's the problem, isn't it?"

"You haven't got a clue," she says.

"My God," he whispers. "What kind of monster have you created?"

"Get out," she says. "Get… just leave. Disappear. Out."

Mark turns on his heel. "No problem." He grabs the Super Girl toy and bounds up the stairs, shouting as he goes. "Out of control! Jessica, *you* are out of control!"

Morning light is too soft for what has just passed.

Mark carries his daughter, Lori, and her tricycle to his Mini Cooper parked in the villas' circular drive. He loads them into the back, careful but quickly. Then he turns to look one last time at the glassed-in Bauhaus mansion.

Resigned, he gets in and pulls out quickly, tires losing tread. He doesn't look back.

Jessica now stands alone in the upper lounge office, surrounded by her memorabilia from years of travel—silent ghosts of her memories.

The neutrinos flicker across her laptop screen like silent prayers to a god she no longer believes in. "I only wanted to eliminate the weapons," she whispers. "I only wanted to move matter. I only wanted…"

But the universe does not answer. It never does.

And somewhere in the silence, the words of J. Robert Oppenheimer rise like smoke from the ashes of history: "Now I am become Death, the destroyer of worlds." She closes her eyes as the quote settles over her like a shroud.

Not yet. Not death. But something close. Something waiting. Something still to be discovered.

THIRTEEN

Ancient ley lines

CORRIDORS OF WHITE STRETCH endlessly through a research facility in China, the quiet hum of machines saturating the sterile air. Overhead, fluorescent lights buzz like distant wasps. Within this labyrinth of secrecy, two men converge: one in the crisp uniform of intelligence, the other draped in a lab coat, his presence almost spectral.

Hui Chen moves with clipped steps, eyes sharp and voice sharper. Beside him, Chow Kia Ho Chief Weapons Scientist keeps pace, his calm gaze belying the storm of thoughts within.

"Ab Barik," Chow begins, voice low, almost reverent. "A fascinating incident."

"I'm not interested in fascination," Hui Chen replies, his tone a blade. "I want understanding."

Chow nods, absorbing the urgency in Hui's stride, the restless twitch of his fingers.

"We've concluded," Chow continues, "that only an orbital laser-driven beam weapon could cause such devastation. But even that would leave residue. Trace elements. Debris."

"And yet," Hui Chen says, narrowing his eyes, "there is nothing. No carbon. No radioactivity. No DNA. How is that possible?"

They push through double doors into a vast, tall chamber lit by windows. The laboratory's chill is broken only by the soft whisper of filtered air.

"My colleagues suspect some form of X-ray beam," Chow says, doubt in his voice. "But I think it's more."

"More?" Hui Chen echoes. "How so? Has such a weapon ever been deployed?"

"Not to our knowledge. Unless there's information hidden even from us." Chow pauses. "Another theory is a fusion bomb—highly energized atomic nuclei, traveling near light speed, striking from orbit. But it doesn't seem feasible."

Hui Chen frowns. "Either it is or it isn't. I trust you can explain."

"It's unlikely," Chow admits. "But we can't rule it out. Not yet."

Chow gestures to a raised platform, where ghostlike assistants wait in silence.

At the center, a transparent demi-sphere, ten feet in diameter, hangs suspended. Inside is a model village set into an area of mountains.

Hui Chen steps closer, his aide trailing behind. Chow joins him, gesturing toward the structure.

"In the 1890s," Chow begins, "Nikola Tesla theorized the existence of ley lines—energy fields capable of conducting electromagnetic force across the planet. Energy that could be shifted, redirected."

He nods to his assistants. The lights dim. Darkness swallows the room. The demi-sphere glows, ethereal. Tendrils of electricity curl around the miniature village like ghostly fingers.

Chow inserts a probe into a control panel. The current tightens, spinning into a vortex. The village shudders, then vanishes sucked into the void. Vaporized. Gone.

"More than illusion," Chow murmurs. "I believe Dr. Jessica Peake has taken Tesla's vision a quantum leap forward. She may have found a way to channel these ley lines, much like our medical practitioners channel Chi."

Chow removes the probe. The lights return. The vortex fades.

Hui Chen raises a brow. "You're saying she used… cosmic acupuncture to destroy men and weapons?"

Chow nods. "Only in this case, her needles appear to be neutrinos."

"Neutrinos?" Hui Chen repeats, the word foreign and sharp on his tongue.

"That's the theory. In the 1960s, three American scientists discovered infinitesimal particles, Neutrinos, that play a fundamental role in the structure of matter. With no electromagnetic charge, they can pass through a wall of lead miles thick."

He taps a console. A hologram of the Earth's core rises, rendered in light with streams of particles passing through it.

Chow stands transfixed, observing the extraordinary image.

"But what if," he continues, "we could give them charge? Direct them? Let them pass through matter, but control their path?"

The hologram shifts. Lines of energy pierce the planet, rebounding, converging.

"It's not just theory, neutrinos do pass through the planet entirely." Chow gestures to the simulation. "We call it the Point Source Hypothesis. I suspect Dr. Peake has learned to harness that energy. Fire it into space. Redirect it. Return it, a loop of destruction."

"A ferocious weapon," Hui Chen murmurs. "Do we have the means to block it? Or the technology to duplicate it?"

Chow hesitates. "No. Not yet. But we're closer than ever. Given time—"

"How much time?" Hui Chen cuts in, voice cold. "I need a number." Hui Chen stands motionless beneath the harsh lights, Chow's words reverberating in his mind. *Neutrinos, particles that pass through everything: lead walls, flesh, the Earth itself. Unseen. Unstoppable. The implications hang in the air like silent, invisible radiation.*

He thinks of the village at Ab Barik now nothing but scorched earth and silence. Not even ashes. As if its people had never lived. As if history itself had been cauterized.

He turns to Chow, voice barely a whisper. "If she can reach through the Earth and back again… then nowhere is beyond her reach."

Chow doesn't answer. He doesn't need to. The warning hangs between them—a meditation on humanity's pursuit of knowledge older and more dangerous than they understand.

The light above flickers, then steadies, white, surgical. Somewhere deep in the facility, a machine exhales. Hui Chen looks back at the demi-sphere, its glass now dark, the vortex gone. But the memory of its hunger remains.

He thinks of Tesla, of Peake, of the ancient ley lines whispering beneath their feet. And for the first time in his long career, Hui Chen feels the chill of something older than war…Not a weapon.

A reckoning.

FOURTEEN

The storm before

The Villa, late afternoon

THE BLADES OF THE BLACK COBRA helicopter carve the sky with sound, descending onto the private helipad like a mechanical predator. The air is thick with salt and heat. Below, Lt. Colonel Clark Ramsey, retired Airborne, spine still rigid with habit, waits in an immaculately styled dark blue pinstriped suit. A jacket that hangs softly from his shoulders and slim-lined cuffed trousers paint the canvas of this man, as he shades his eyes against the glare.

The Vice President arrives without ceremony. Douglas Mallory steps down onto the tarmac in a dark shirt, open at the collar, jacket flapping slightly in the rotor wash. No tie. No pretense. Just the weight of Washington behind his stride. Secret Service agents fan out around him like shadows. Ramsey salutes. Mallory returns it without eye contact.

In the subterranean sanctum of Atlantis, Jessica Peake watches the blue warning light flash above the console. She's dressed in slim, well-washed Levi's jeans and a button-down shirt, her hair tied back, and her eyes alert.

Maggie's face flickers onto the screen, all wit and warning. "Dr. Peake, you have a visitor—Vice President Douglas Mallory, in all his glory."

Jessica doesn't flinch. She presses a panel and her chair detaches, gliding along a recessed rail to the far end of the control room.

Above, in the studio, the ceiling opens. The chair rises and she steps off, crosses into the upper office, and walks through the double doors into the reception lounge.

Mallory is already there. He stands before a tall wall of triple-glazed glass, gazing out at the ocean, the mountains, and the green lushness of the island. In the distance, storm clouds gather, like a shadow over his thoughts.

"Splendid view," he says, dabbing his brow with a white handkerchief. "But you've got a storm front coming. And not a pretty one."

Jessica's voice is calm, precise. "And yet you're willing to brave the elements. Must be important."

He sniffs at a flower arrangement, as if searching for something human in the sterile beauty. "I hear you once used your neutrino tech to vanish a conch shell at Jones Beach."

"Part of Holst's *The Planets*," she replies. "Neptune. The Magician. But I brought it back in the final movement."

Mallory turns, eyes narrowing. "But not the finale at Ab Barik? Seems we've lost an entire village, including twenty-eight NATO Rangers. Care to tell me what the hell happened?"

Jessica's gaze doesn't flinch. "Not sure I can. Not yet. I apologize for the inconvenience."

"*Inconvenience?*" His voice rises, sharp with fury. "I trust you're being ironic. Russia, China, the EU, they're all sniffing up our ass. And don't look now, but I'm the best friend you've got."

Jessica crosses the room, pours herself a glass of water with deliberate, measured movements. "Walter Hamilton is my friend. You're a money source."

Mallory laughs, bitter. "And a damned good one. When Congress defunded you for non-performance, I got you what you needed. No red tape. No oversight. At no small risk to myself."

"No red tape?" she scoffs. "From the Consortium? They're Mephistopheles with a boner. Talk about a Faustian pact."

He shrugs. "One we're both caught in. And if I'm fucked, believe me, so are you."

She sits on the arm of a chair, eyes on the storm outside. She gestures for him to pour his own water. "There was supposed to be no pressure." She takes a drink.

"There wasn't," Mallory growls. "For two years, there was nothing but patience. Now there's pressure. And rumors that others have the technology... China!"

"Not at this level they don't," she snaps back. "With rising tensions, nations may rely more on cyberattacks and the evolved AI-driven defense systems. We have a world of uncertainty, misinformation, and digital sabotage."

Mallory's eyes narrow. "I believe you. So does the Royal Swedish Academy of Science. They say your physics are beyond anything known. As a deterrent, this could end war as we know it."

Jessica sets her glass aside, her gaze hardening. "Then give it time, Doug. It's nowhere near ready to fill its ultimate purpose application." She raises her voice, letting it ring. *"Peace!"*

Mallory's voice hardens. "Fuck its ultimate purpose. We need it now. As a hammer, so we can bring this arms race madness to an end before we blow up the entire fucking world."

He breathes out, reins himself in. "So, bring your schematics when you come to Washington. We'll get you re-funded."

Jessica rises, loosens her hair, walks to the terrace. The glass doors part as she steps into the rising wind. "Schematics?" she says, incredulous. "They won't even know what they're looking at."

Mallory follows, jacket snapping in the wind. "Exactly."

The sky is bruised and trembling. Her hair is whipped by the coming storm. The waters of the ocean merge with the grey dark sheets of rain.

Jessica looks back at him, her tone shifting, the weight of history pressing between them. "Do you ever think about how many wars have raged since the atom bomb was meant to end them? We're still tangled in global crises—climate denial, famine, families fleeing horrors in their homelands. Pollution, too, still unresolved."

Mallory's expression grows distant, almost philosophical. "The problem isn't the deterrent, Jessica. It's in the hearts of those who believe they control the world."

She meets his gaze, unflinching.

"Don't worry about my heart, Peake. Focus on the mind we purchased. Remember? You belong to us now."

Jessica's lips curl in a faint, bitter smile. "Every sweet promise is a razor's edge. One word from me, and you might as well tie the traitor's noose yourself, it's waiting for you."

Mallory's tone is cold. "Is that a threat? Don't bother. One way or another, we'll get what we paid for."

She feels a flicker of unease but masks it. "You're a master of subtlety, aren't you?"

He leans in, voice low. "The Investigating Committee will have questions tomorrow. I suggest you find some Machiavellian answers." He turns to go, then pauses at the door. "And again, don't forget the blueprint, for the President. Make sure it's ready, genius."

Jessica watches him go, her wariness growing. "See yourself out, Mr. Vice President."

Mallory nods, muttering to himself. "Of course, you'll have it ready. You need the money."

She stands on the terrace, wind whipping around her, staring into the storm's heart. "And the Consortium?" she calls after him.

Mallory, without turning, says, "I'll handle them."

"No," she says quietly. "They're handling you. You're playing both ends against the middle. And it will be the end of you."

Mallory doesn't blink. "You underrate me. Everyone does."

"And you're underestimating this storm." Her voice is low, almost kind. "So, I suggest you get on your horse."

Mallory's silhouette fades into the darkness. "Friday. Ten a.m. Be there."

Jessica stands alone, the storm gathering its strength, the world outside as uncertain as the one within.

Ramsey is holding a large black umbrella, waiting on the steps of the villa. This time, Mallory acknowledges him. "Make certain nothing happens to her between now and Washington, Ramsey."

Mallory is escorted to the waiting Jeep.

The Cobra lifts off moments later, slicing through the growing storm, heading east toward Saint Kitts.

Jessica stands alone on the balcony, drenched now, her eyes on the crashing waves below. Thunder rumbles. The sea claws at the seawall, relentless. The storm is never just weather. It is the shadow of consequence, gathering at the edges of ambition.

She stands at the threshold between science and power, between control and compromise. Mallory comes not as a villain, but as a man already caught in the machinery, desperate, cornered, wearing civility like armor. His hands are outstretched, but not for peace. Not yet.

Jessica's technology, like Prometheus' fire, was never meant to be a weapon. But in the hands of those who fear the dark, even light becomes a threat.

And so, the storm arrives. Not with thunder alone, but with questions. What price is truth when wrapped in secrecy? What good is peace when it must be forced? And how long can one stand on the edge of invention before the world demands a leap? In the distance, the waves rise…and the world waits.

FIFTEEN

The river remembers

THE CHARLES RIVER SHIMMERED like polished glass beneath a sky brushed in watercolor blues. Morning mist curled around the banks, whispering secrets to the reeds. And then a crack, a slap, a rhythm. A pulse.

Eight oars struck the water in perfect, percussive unity. Eight women, strong and synchronized, pulled against the current, their breath rising and falling like a single living creature. The coxswain's voice cut through the air, sharp, commanding, urgent as the lightweight Harvard women's crew surged forward.

The female cox made a command. "Remember the Roman Galley. Breathe one breath together," she shouted. "Now!"

As one with eight combined breaths, the blades, with full force, pulled the narrow craft high through the waters of the river's fast current.

Jessica Peake, in her early twenties, sat in the sixth seat, muscles taut, face set in fierce concentration. Her world had narrowed to the beat of the blades and the fire in her lungs. The regatta was in full cry, Harvard versus Yale—ancient rivals locked in aquatic ballet. The shells skimmed the surface like dragonflies, neck and neck, slicing through time.

On the riverbank, a crowd roared a chorus of human thunder. Among them, Sir Anthony Wood, elegant in his tweed and timelessness walked with calm detachment, his gait unconsciously echoing the rhythm of the rowers. Nearby, Mark Richards, all youthful charm and fervent devotion, cupped his hands and called out, "Jessica! Jessica! Jessica!" Her name was a war cry and a love song.

Jessica's body screamed with effort, but she did not falter. Stroke for stroke, breath for breath, she and her sisters in the boat gave everything they had. And then in one final surge, their shell lifted, leapt, and crossed the finish line by the tip of a bow. Victory, by less than a yard.

A sigh, collective and cathartic, rose from both boats. Some women collapsed forward, others fell back, eyes skyward, hearts thundering. Jessica's shell drifted beneath the bridge, gliding from shadow into light.

The Longfellow Bar near Harvard Square welcomed them like a cathedral of celebration. The victorious crew poured in, radiant and reborn, their presence igniting the room. A Queen anthem rose from the crowd, "We Are the Champions"—a secular hymn of triumph.

Jessica, now clean and luminous in her post-race glow, was flanked by two men: Mark Richards on one side, Sir Anthony Wood on the other.

"The world loves a winner," Mark said, pressing a kiss to her cheek.

"And here I am," Jessica replied, looping her arms through theirs, "flanked by my two favorite men: Mark Richards and Nobel Laureate Sir Anthony Wood!"

"Ah, the Nobel Prize for quixotic gestures," Sir Anthony quipped, ever the self-deprecating knight.

"For your relentless defense and rescue of religious minorities persecuted in Chinese Asia," Jessica countered, her tone reverent. "I am humbled in your presence."

"Ah, humility," he mused. "Part of her hidden charm."

"Part of her mortal disguise," Mark added with a grin.

The trio laughed, their glasses clinking in a toast to the moment, to youth, to victory, to possibility.

Later, as the night thinned and the music faded, Jessica and Sir Anthony stood at the bar, deep in quiet conversation. Mark held court with fraternity brothers in the corner, but Jessica's mind was elsewhere. Already rowing toward the future.

"You captained brilliantly today," Sir Anthony said. "Ever consider the Olympics?"

"With single sculls, perhaps. Or pairs. Never the eights. Too much room for weakness."

"Forever the elitist," he teased.

"No! A realist. I work better alone."

"No one works alone when it comes down to it," he said. "We're all merely pieces in the Great Puzzle, trying somehow to fit. The question is where?"

"I know where I fit," she said, her voice steady. "I want to continue my research with you when you move to MIT."

He studied her carefully. "Why follow me? Time to chart your own path. Create your own mythology or be slave to another man's."

"William Blake," she replied. "I know what he meant. My mythology is particle physics. Neutrino research."

"Ah, neutrinos," he said, eyes twinkling. "Ghost particles of the universe. In everything. Of nothing. No charge, no purpose."

"But what if I could find a charge?" she asked. "Or give them one?"

He smiled. "Then you might become the Creator God of a new Eden…or Shiva, the Destroyer of Worlds."

"With great risk comes great reward." A quick, hardened reaction from Jessica.

"Or a lifetime of frustration," he warned. "Be careful what you wish for, my young Padawan. You just might get it."

"I will pursue it," she said, "with no remorse."

"Then apply the Irenic Principle when you do. That which is designed to create peace in the world."

"For neutrino research?" she laughed. "How would that ever lead to peace?"

"Well, that is your quest, isn't it?" he said softly. "And therein lies your Grail."

Across the room, Mark called out again, his voice cutting through the reverie. "Jessica! Jessica!"

She turned, caught between two worlds. The one that adored her, and the one she was destined to discover.

With a martini clasped in her hand, those memories of her college days drifted in and out between sips of the Hendrick's gin.

The Charles River, winding through the heart of Cambridge, was more than a backdrop for her rowing. In literature, rivers often symbolize change, time, and transformation. The Charles became both a literal arena of competition and a metaphorical current. One that carried her from the restless energy of youth into the quiet momentum of purpose.

The coxswain's voice, a sharp, unseen presence, guides the rhythm of the boat, but it also mirrored her own internal compass. Just as the cox steers the crew with calm authority, so too did she begin to hear the emerging voice of her ambition, preparing to navigate the complexities of her scientific path.

Sir Anthony Wood entered the narrative as a composite figure: part mentor part provocateur. He evoked the archetype of the wise guide, yet he also challenged her assumptions, refusing to offer easy answers. In this way, he became a kind of Dumbledore with the intellectual gravity of an Oppenheimer—brilliant, enigmatic, and morally ambiguous.

The introduction of the Irenic Principle from the Greek *eirēnikos,* meaning peace-making, marked a turning point in her understanding of science. No longer was her research a purely intellectual endeavor; it now carried ethical weight. The principle suggests that knowledge, at its highest level, must be tempered by a responsibility to heal rather than harm.

Now, Neutrinos, those elusive subatomic particles that pass through matter almost undetected, became a fitting metaphor for herself. Like them, she moved quietly through the academic world, underestimated and unseen, yet charged with potential. Her journey, much like theirs, defied easy detection but carried immense significance.

All these thoughts now that I've been summoned to Washington. Am I ready? She snuggled into the comfort of the large sofa cushions, caught up in her thoughts, questioning.

At the heart of my transformation is a call to create my own mythology. A direct echo of William Blake's radical vision. I stand at a crossroads, caught between the safety of my established paths and the uncertainty of forging my own. She raised the glass and, in one gulp, emptied it. Her decision would shape not only her career but the very essence of who she would become. Her eyes closed, the empty glass slowly leaving her limp hand.

Tonight, the duality of Shiva the Hindu god who is both destroyer and creator casts a long shadow over Jessica's ambition. In physics, as in mythology, creation and destruction are intertwined. Jessica's work holds the promise of discovery, but also the peril of unintended consequences, a tension that will only deepen.

SIXTEEN

The veil is lifting

THE NIGHT PASSED AS a tapestry of rain and memory. The following morning, Jessica stood alone on her balcony, winds tugging at her thoughts of the previous night and Mallory's visit. Her phone vibrated against the railing, screen flickering with the ghost of a FaceTime call.

Taylor's face shimmered through the static like a signal lost in deep space. "Jessica! Jessica! We've got to talk!"

She blinked, surfacing from the depths of recollection. The voice was urgent, fractured by distance. "John, you're breaking up… badly."

Then, silence. A pause. And finally, a voice more determined than distorted.

"Never mind. I'm on my way over."

Outside, the storm gathered its breath. The rain came down in sheets, hammering the villa complex with monsoon fury. Taylor's red Jeep Wrangler churned through the downpour. Although it was daytime, its headlights cut jagged lines through the gloom. It skidded to a halt at the gates, the engine growling like a caged animal.

Inside the security center, an overweight, bearded security guard sat in front of a table with a small glass of dark rum, reading a smut magazine. He looked up through the window as Taylor continued to honk the horn.

Angrily, the sergeant, having spotted the vehicle and Taylor, shouted, "Taylor, you impatient shit!"

He got up, spilling the glass of rum, cursing all the way to press the button that opened the gates. He waved him through without hesitation as the gates groaned open, definitely needed oiling.

Thunder cracked like the voice of something ancient and unseen. Jessica was already waiting in the doorway, just beyond the reach of the rain. Taylor leapt from the Jeep, instantly soaked to the bone, a weatherproof portfolio clutched beneath his arm like a sacred text.

"I couldn't get through to you," he panted. "Where have you been? I couldn't shut down the fusion valve."

Taylor opened the wet portfolio and pulled out three sheets of printed records.

Jessica snatched the sheets from his hands, her eyes scanning the data like a codebreaker reading a prophecy. Without a word, she grabbed Taylor's arm and pulled him toward the Jeep.

"Read it to me," she commanded, sliding behind the wheel.

The Wrangler fishtailed across the slick cobblestones, tires slicing through the floodwaters as the gates yawned open. With the guard standing in total disbelief in the open door of the security center, they sped through the drenched countryside's narrow roads. Torrential streams poured from the hillsides, as the Wrangler skidded past fallen palms scattered in its path.

"The neutrino count is off the hook!" Taylor shouted over the roar of the rain.

"I got that much. How many?"

"Look!" He held up a trembling page. "Just look!"

Jessica's eyes widened as he thrust the sheet in front of her. "What? How can this be real? That star must have been enormous." She grabbed for the data, nearly veering off the road.

"Just get us there alive, will you?" Taylor barked pulling sheets away from her.

Jessica's voice dropped, reverent. "The supernova would have quadrupled the neutrino count. Enhanced the propagator to the fifteenth joule! Maybe beyond."

"Then why didn't the fusion intake valve close? The tritium temperature was constant, thirty degrees Celsius above absolute zero."

Jessica's breath caught. "That's more than we've ever captured, even in the Antarctic plugs. But the question is, why didn't it register when I checked? Unless—"

"A veil. The heat is a veil," Taylor said, catching her thought midair.

"Disguising the real activity," she finished. "Exactly."

The Neutrino Trap Hangar emerged from the hillside like a mythic temple set into the mountainside, its domed silhouette glowing faintly through the downpour.

"All these external influences…it's got to be more than just quantitative!" Jessica screamed to Taylor, who flinched at her shrillness.

The Jeep skidded to a halt, tires spraying arcs of water. They ran through the storm, Taylor pressing his eye to the biometric scanner. The massive metallic door groaned open, revealing the red-lit cathedral of science within—the walls only hinting at the mysterious quantum dance unfolding within.

Inside, the hangar that stretched six stories high had been carved out of and into the mountain. Metal walkways threaded overhead like veins. Jessica and Taylor scaled the ladder, cutting off emergency lights as they moved toward the core.

The Neutrino Trap Housing pulsed with light and warning tones. HDR readouts blinked erratically. Jessica moved with precision, her hands dancing across control panels as she tried to cut off the power.

"The fusion valve is locked open," she muttered. "Stay here. I'm going into the Collection Chamber. Make certain the intake valves are sealed."

Donning a radiation-blocking jacket, Jessica crossed the gantry and disappeared through a sealed door, leaving Taylor at the control panel, his fingers dancing over keys as he monitored the chaotic patterns. The Collection Chamber was a sanctuary of silence. Jessica placed her hand on a scanner set into the wall; the door slid open, and she descended into the silence of the heart of her creation

Jessica's Collection Chamber was a marvel. An immense, twenty-foot-diameter metal Globe, the sanctuary was nestled within a shadowy cavern that watched the darkness like a thousand curious eyes. Within the Globe, pure water glowed faintly, awaiting the rarest of visitors: a neutrino.

The Quantum Dance. Invisible threads of energy, like ghostly dancers, wove silently through the Globe's heart. Their presence was betrayed only by the occasional burst of ethereal blue light. A Cherenkov ring flared into existence as a neutrino brushed the edge of the quantum world. Abstract patterns of swirling energy rippled across the inner walls, hinting at the mysterious dance unfolding within.

The sense of the unseen was everywhere: neutrinos, elusive, almost mythical. Passed effortlessly through stone, steel, and soul, their journey a cosmic ballet connecting Jessica's chamber to the vastness of the universe itself.

Metal stairways led to walkways crisscrossing the high ceiling, converging at the heart of the steel globe suspended in a cradle of massive titanium tubes. Its surface shimmered with the ghost-light of a thousand reactions. Beneath the glass floor, the particle accelerator hummed like a sleeping dragon. She ascended to the base of the globe and pressed her face to one of the protective screens.

Inside, light danced. A revelation, trillions of particles in ecstatic motion, expanding and contracting in patterns that defied language. Her breath caught. Something shifted within her: agony, ecstasy, revelation.

"At last," she whispered. "Thank God… at last."

Taylor took her hand as she exited the Collection Chamber, noting the change in her demeanor and the awareness that seemed to have come with her transformed expression. With growing unease, he said, "Something happened back there. Want to clue me in?" Witnessing her anxiousness, he waited for her answer.

Jessica turned to him, eyes alight. "The overload wasn't an accident. There was a plan. John, they were trying to communicate with us. I'm sure of it. We need to reverse the process."

He stared at her. "You're serious? We agreed that thirty degrees Celsius maximizes activity."

"We need to reverse the process. Thirty degrees above absolute zero maximizes activity, yes—but it also accelerates decay. We've been burning the message before we could read it."

"And if we go the other direction?" John asked.

"Lower it. Thirty degrees below absolute zero. Like the Ice Cube in Antarctica, which will render them inert."

"And when we're ready?"

"We raise the temperature slowly. Harvest them. Shape the signal." She leaned against the chamber wall, the weight of realization pressing down on her.

"Oh, my God," she breathed. "I've had it all wrong up to now."

Outside, the storm raged on. But inside the chamber, something had shifted, something fundamental. The veil was lifting. The silence was speaking. And Jessica, for the first time, was ready to listen. She remembered the poem her mother would often recite to her at bed time:

> *When the curtain falls and the lights grow dim,*
> *The echoes linger of a half-sung hymn.*
> *Pages turned, the tale complete,*
> *Yet in the silence, hearts still beat.*
> *Footsteps fade on a twilight stage,*
> *Whispers written on time's last page.*
> *Not an ending, but a gentle sigh—*
> *A promise tucked in a star-strewn sky.*
> *So let the song drift soft and low,*
> *A memory wrapped in afterglow.*
> *For every story, though it ends,*
> *Leaves a tune the soul defends.*

SEVENTEEN

The light that listens

THE STORM HAD PASSED, but its breath still lingers, long fingers of wind tapping insistently against the villa's glass. Jessica, back in the villa, stands alone in the control center, the heart of Atlantis humming around her. The air is thick with ozone and revelation. She takes a couple of sticks of her favorite incense and lights them, wafting the smoke around the console, then places it safely in the holder, then pulls the chair towards her and sits.

Her hands dart over the console with practiced urgency. As she works, holographic projections bloom into existence, each one unfolding with greater complexity than the one before.

They are visions of the Neutrino field. Captured data from the Propagator, now reanimated in ghostly light. She watches them bloom and collapse, galaxies born and devoured in moments. The particles multiply, trillions folding into themselves, then exploding outward again. A cosmic breath. A silent scream.

Then something shifts.

A face emerges from the storm of data. Mark Richards. His image oscillates with a strange frequency—half-light, half-memory. Behind him, the face of a young boy from Ab Barik his eyes wide, his mouth open in terror flickers into view. He vanishes in a shimmer of disintegration.

And then, Mark's voice, echoing from the void: "What kind of monster have you created? *You...you created...*"

The words reverberate through her chest. The room tilts. The holograms take on a life of their own, no longer simulations but something autonomous, something aware.

They swirl around her, particles dancing like spirits, like accusations. She sees the boy again. His eyes. His fear. His mother's outstretched hand, fading. Jessica gasps.

The air thickens. The energy turns hostile. She can't breathe. Her hand slams down on the console, not from thought but reflex. The screens freeze locking onto the boy's face in a moment of pure agony.

The rods of the console begin to glow, their light swelling in gentle waves. Jessica stares, transfixed, as if caught between breaths. Her hands move again slower now, more deliberate, as though she is listening for a music only she can hear. She enters a sequence of equations drawn from sacred geometry, patterns she's only glimpsed in dreams, each symbol a prayer, each line a whisper of something beyond words.

The equations resist her at first, trembling at her touch, then yield softening, unfolding. Something ancient stirs in the quiet, a hush that is both invitation and promise. A halo of light forms above her, luminous and serene. She pushes away from the console, steps back, startled, but the light draws her in with gentle insistence. It pulses with intelligence. It sees her. It knows her, as if it has always known her.

And then she is no longer consciously in the room. Her body lifts...or dissolves, she cannot tell. Her awareness stretches, unfurling like a sail in a silent wind.

She rises through the villa, beyond the island, up through the clouds and far above the Earth, which spins beneath her, small and blue and impossibly fragile. She soars higher still, traveling beyond stars, consciously weaving her way through the solar system.

Twelve solar systems pass beneath her, encircling twelve more colossal star systems, each more expansive, more luminous than the last. Then twelve more, unfolding like petals of a cosmic flower. She is pulled toward the center of something vast, something that breathes with a holiness beyond language. Galaxies spiral like clockwork around a central iris of light. She enters it, surrendering.

Darkness. Not absence, but presence—an infinite blackness filled with shimmering threads of light, each one a thought, a possibility, a hope. Quintillions of light particles dance in arcs before her, interweaving, separating into ellipses, spinning counterclockwise. Electric charges surge. Chaos blooms, yet within it, a profound order, a peace that passes understanding.

She is translucent, diaphanous, pure awareness adrift on a sea of wonder. Before her, a wall of trillions of neutrinos absorbs the pure energy of nothingness. They spin, creating an electrical charge, separating, colliding, merging with the counter-spin. The union births a vision: a man and a woman, naked and radiant, birthed before her, straddling the Earth. Neutrinos pass through them, through the planet, through time itself—a chain of consciousness, a cosmic breath.

The light fades. It is dawn. Jessica slumps forward on the console, returned to her body. The lab still pulses with residual energy. Holograms self-assemble before her, systems within systems, each one singing softly of an eternal connection. She is drained. Changed.

The silence that follows is not emptiness, but fulfillment. She lifts her head and calls John Taylor. His image appears on the screen, his hair tousled, a mug of coffee in hand. His voice is tight with concern.

"God, I'm glad it's you," he says. "I couldn't sleep."

Jessica smiles faintly, she is remembering, her voice hoarse but steady. "John, you won't believe what I've just experienced."

He waits.

She freezes mid-motion, her eyes widening as the realization strikes. "Wait," she breathes, her voice trembling with awe. "I know what we've been missing." The room seems to hold its breath. "What if…what if all this time, everything we've been searching for, all the experiments, the anomalies, what if it's been right in front of us?" She leans forward, her hands gripping the edge of the console. "Those minute, elusive buggers—the neutrinos. We've always thought of them as just particles, as fleeting messengers from the stars. But what if they're more than that? What if they are consciousness itself? Neutrinos are consciousness! Billions of them passing through us every second!"

Her words hang in the air, electric with possibility, as the implications ripple through her and John Taylor.

She takes a moment as she continues to remember. "They are like a screen that primal conscious comes through. Let's say the prime source of creation. By being able to collect them, we are able to have the raw energy of spontaneous creation.

"John does that make sense? That is the energy behind it…It's the energy that propels particles into bigger building blocks of life that then become atoms and molecules and larger life forms in the Universe."

He stares at her from the screen, silent.

"We've been trying to manipulate them like tools," she continues. But they're not passive. They're not inert. They're the building blocks of everything." She takes a pause. "And, John, they're trying to speak to us."

John leans forward. "You're saying we can enhance them? Make them think?"

"I'm saying they already do," Jessica says, her voice thick with wonder. "And they want to help us to evolve." She hesitates. "Maybe, no not evolve, they're here to guide us."

John shakes his head, half in disbelief. "You're talking about something science hasn't even touched on in a millennium—has no understanding of. Ever!"

"I know," she says. "And that's exactly why we're ready."

He narrows his eyes. "So... how?"

Jessica leans back, smiling through the exhaustion. "I have no idea, John." She laughs, then breathes in, the light still humming beneath her skin.

"And that," she says, "is the perfect place to start." She laughs even louder, then touches the console, commanding her chair to track across the control area, lock into a shaft close to the elevator and rise up into the upper office.

The chamber stood empty now. Where once voices clashed and visions vied for dominance, only silence remained, dignified, patient, and resolute. Jessica, newly awakened, walked the corridor alone, her footsteps echoing softly across polished marble floors each step a gentle ripple in the hush. It was time for a rest.

EIGHTEEN

Jade Spring Hill, Beijing

THE STARS OVER BEIJING blinked dimly through the haze of city light, but from the roof garden of the Jade Spring Hill Palace, the skyline shimmered like a promise. Premier Yang Bing Rong stood alone beside a brass-mounted telescope, his hands clasped lightly behind his back as he observed the stars

The night air was cool, scented faintly with Sweet Osmanthus, Yang's favorite aroma. Below, the city shimmered and pulsed with quiet urgency. Tall elegant architectural wonders of design seemed to float above the city haze.

Behind him, Deputy Chief Ben Hui Chen waited, still and formal, a thick folder tucked beneath one arm like a sealed verdict.

"Mr. Chairman," Hui Chen said quietly.

Yang didn't turn. "Yes, Director. I read the Jessica Peake file."

He adjusted the telescope a fraction, as though seeking clarity not just in the stars, but in the uncertain alignments of power and technology.

"Exceptional work, if it holds," he continued. "Which, as we know, it has yet to do. Our R&D is a year behind her in the same field of neutrino development."

"At least," Hui Chen confirmed.

"Does anyone else have command of this?"

His eye still fixed within the lens of the telescope, he responded, "According to our intelligence, no. We're a close second. But second nonetheless."

Yang finally turned, his eyes narrowing not in anger, but in calculation. "This is not the Olympics. There are no silver medals for second place." He stepped away from the telescope, the weight of the night pressing in.

"Our people need more time," he said, almost gently. "And apparently, Dr. Peake is the sole impediment."

"Apparently," Hui Chen agreed and bowed.

Yang's voice dropped to a whisper, but it carried like a sentence handed down. "Then remove the impediment."

Hui Chen bowed again, stepping back into the shadows, the folder still unopened. Yang returned to his telescope, but his gaze had turned inward now, fixed not on the stars, but on the shape of what must be done.

Shanghai, midday

In the ultra-modern, futuristic city, the rooftop garden of the high-rise was a fusion of elegance and edge—glass fountains, polished stone, and the glint of chrome. A photo shoot was in progress. The model, a tall, feline, statuesque Chinese woman, moved with a grace that was both art and artifice. She wore a stunning, fashion-forward storm-gray jacket, slim-cut slacks, and boots. The photographer, a tall, handsome Cantonese man, moved around with his digital camera, snapping photos as the model shifted position—his lens capturing not just her shape, but her precision.

She circled two other models that flanked the fountain, props in a tableau of urban couture. The tall Chinese model toyed with each of the other girls flirtatiously, moving in and out and posing herself like a cat.

Then, without warning, the scene shifted. The photographer's hand flicked. The lens cap became a shuriken, slicing through the air and into one of the model's foreheads with a crack that echoed off the marble. The other model barely had time to move before the Chinese model's silver necklace, with blinding speed, flashed through the air wrapping, tightening and creating a garrote with such force that it decapitated the young model's head. As the head rolled, silence returned.

Ben Hui Chen stepped through a side door, the envelope already in his hand. He did not flinch at the shattered models or the quiet violence that seemed to linger in the air.

"I'm impressed. I have an assignment for you both," he said.

The photographer, on seeing his chairman, bowed and then took the envelope, opening it with a flick. The model leaned in, seeing names. Coordinates. A face.

"Time and place?" the photographer asked.

The model smiled. She already knew.

Hui Chen's voice was calm. "Two birds with one stone."

The pair exchanged a glance, professional, intimate, lethal. The mission was clear.

Somewhere far from the glinting rooftops and silent telescopes, Dr. Jessica Peake continued her work, unaware that the calculus of power had shifted, and that she was now the variable to be eliminated.

Peace, when threatened, often reveals the sharpened blade beneath diplomacy's silk glove

NINETEEN

The arrival

DUSK DRAPED ITSELF ACROSS the tarmac like a velvet curtain as Jessica Peake's Learjet rolled to a smooth halt beside the Landmark Aviation hangar. The jet's sleek silhouette cut through the fading light, its engines whispering into silence.

Waiting below, tall and composed, stood a man carved from the same granite as the monuments of this city. Special Agent Jason Wells. He was in his mid-fifties, silver at the temples, and looked tailored in a charcoal three-piece suit that spoke of quiet authority. His eyes, sharp and blue, scanned the descending figure.

Jessica emerged, indigo pantsuit crisp against the golden hour, a green Il Bisonte attaché case swinging from her hand like a sword in its sheath. Her heels tapped lightly on the metal stairs as she descended.

"Dr. Peake," Wells said, offering his hand. "I'm Agent Jason Wells. I've been assigned to escort you during your time in Washington... and to all points thereafter."

Jessica paused, her eyes narrowing slightly. Then, with a diplomat's grace, she extended her hand. Their shake was brief but weighted.

"I appreciate the attention," she said coolly. "But is all this really necessary?"

Wells gestured toward the waiting black Lincoln Town Car, sleek and silent like a panther in waiting.

"President Hamilton thinks it is."

Jessica slid into the back seat, the leather interior sighing beneath her. Wells followed, taking the jump seat across from her.

"So," she said, settling in, "may I inquire as to what branch of the Deep State you're with?"

Wells smiled faintly. "Deep State always sounds so... pejorative. Let's say it's a special branch of the Secret Service."

Jessica smiled. "Oh? Like the 'secret' Secret Service?"

"Something like that. Executive Order. From the man himself."

"You know I have my own security."

"Back on your island, yes. But this is a different level."

Jessica turned to look through the rear windshield. Two black SUVs followed in tight formation, their windows opaque, their presence unmistakable.

"Is all this ours?"

Wells glanced back. "Yes, it is."

Jessica shook her head, almost smiling. "I feel safer already. Now, are you going to be in my face 24/7 for the foreseeable future? Love your subtlety."

Wells quietly responds. "Quite the contrary. You won't even know I'm there until you need me."

The Capitol Dome gleamed in the afternoon sun, its shadow stretching long across the marble steps. Shadows of hidden past chaos. Inside, in Room 321, the Senate Subcommittee on Science and Defense had gathered. Five senators were seated on a dais like judges of fate. A Sub-Council Senate Appropriations Committee. Among them were Senators Jethro Woodbine of Georgia, Charles

Gabriel of Rhode Island, Selina Ramirez of New Mexico, and Myron Polisky of New York.

As the room buzzed with press, aides, and the quiet hum of restrained tension, they were joined by Deputy Defense Secretary Hamm.

Jessica sat alone at a table, a bank of microphones arrayed before her like the barrels of a firing squad with her facing the inquisition.

Senator Charles Gabriel, portly and pale, opened the session. "Dr. Peake, this is an informal hearing, open to the public. You're here before the Science Subcommittee."

"Science and Defense," corrected Senator Woodbine with a drawl.

Gabriel nodded. "Science and Defense. We've received a rather... generous funding request, a bill on your behalf of $1.5 billion. And we're not quite sure what it's for. You've been less than specific."

Senator Ramirez leaned forward, her voice sharp. "You list 'Neutrino Research and Cultivation' without a breakdown. That's more than sketchy, to say the least."

Senator Polisky, urbane and skeptical, added, "With all due respect, Dr. Peake, we're already drowning in neutrino research. The Ice Cube project in Antarctica, DUNE in North Dakota, all with funding that seems to languish in theory for ten-year blocks of time."

Jessica cut in, calm but firm. "The Deep Underground Neutrino Experiment. I'm well aware."

"All these projects do is ask for more research," Polisky said. "More time. More money."

Jessica met his gaze. "Mine is different. Mine harnesses the energy of neutrinos. And puts them to work."

Woodbine leaned in, his voice heavy with implication. "But in what way, Dr. Peake? We actually cut your funding three years ago, did we not?"

"You did."

"And yet you apparently went ahead and latched on to a rather sizable sum from an undisclosed 'private source.' Did you not?"

"Which is my right."

Woodbine's tone sharpened. "Is it also your right to get your 'research' entangled in one of the worst combat disasters in fifty years?" He checks the name. Leans forward. "Ab Barik, Dr. Peak! Ring a bell?"

Jessica's jaw tightened. "Is that a question, Senator, or an accusation?"

Woodbine pressed on. "I mean, that was you're doing, wasn't it? A village evaporated. Villagers, NATO and IS troops gone. No bodies. No wreckage. Just...nothing. This has managed to get the United States and NATO tagged with what might well be considered a war crime. And somehow, your name is in the footnotes."

Jessica's voice rose, not in anger, but in conviction. "War crimes? You want to talk about war crimes? We, as a nation, in our past have been complicit in many war crimes." She takes a long moment, then continues, "Vietnam: 59,000 Americans dead. Five million Vietnamese. Iraq: 7,000 U.S. lives, 450,000 Iraqis. And you come for me over a rumor?"

Gabriel's voice cut through the tension. "That's the past! It's a fair question, Dr. Peake. Yes or no?"

Jessica inhaled. Her voice softened, but her words struck like a bell. "There is no evidence of murder. No signs of mayhem. It was as if they were...transported. Not killed. Not destroyed. Just... gone."

"And did you have anything to do with it?" Woodbine asked.

Jessica's answer came without hesitation. "Yes. And no."

Ramirez pounced. "That's equivocation."

"I'm required to give you nothing, Senator. I'm not your employee. I'm here at the request of the President."

Woodbine scoffed. "So, you're taking the Fifth?"

Jessica stood, her voice rising like a tide. "What's unprecedented, Senator, is my technology. What I've built has the power to end war, to stop destruction before it begins. It is life-changing. World-changing. And I will defend it with my life."

A hush fell over the room.

Senator Polisky leaned forward, his voice low but cutting. "You're telling us you've found a way to trap neutrinos? The same particles that pass through the Earth like it's tissue paper. And pull energy from them?"

He paused, letting the incredulity settle.

"Dr. Peake, either you've cracked the biggest physics breakthrough since Einstein, or you're selling us a science fiction novel with a government grant attached."

Jessica didn't blink. "Senators, I understand your skepticism. Neutrinos are elusive. They pass through planets, people, steel, without a trace. That's the nature of these interacting particles. But what if that changed?"

She stepped forward, her voice steady, almost reverent. "We've developed a containment matrix. Layered graphene. Synthetic muon traps. It slows neutrinos just long enough to tap their oscillations—their energy. This isn't theory. We've powered systems. Briefly, yes: but it's real. It's only the beginning." She pauses. "In case you don't know what a Muon is, it is a subatomic particle that's unstable and decays into other particles, primarily electrons and neutrinos. If any of you are physicists, you will know they are used in various experiments and applications."

She met each of their eyes in turn. "I'm not asking for belief. I'm offering a demonstration."

Polisky leaned back, arms crossed. "If your experiment is the game-changer you say it is... show us. I think that's a fair request."

Jessica allowed herself a small smile. "It is. But it won't be cheap."

Polisky smirked. "I think we can handle it," said tightly as the pencil he held behind his back so in his left hand finally snapped.

Jessica, calm in her immaculate way, her face a mask carved from resolve, descended into the waiting chaos. A river of voices and flashing bulbs. The air was thick with ambition and accusation. A reporter surged forward, microphone thrust like a weapon.

"Dr. Peake, it's rumored you've violated the Strategic Arms Limitation Treaty. Is there any truth to the rumor?"

Jessicas eyes flickered, cool blue steel in the dusk. "None whatsoever," she replied, her voice measured, unhurried. "The Russians were accused in 1986, by the Reagan Administration, of violating the SALT pact."

She moved through the knot of reporters, stride unbroken, their questions snapping at her heels like stray dogs.

She paused, half-turned, observing Wells holding the door of the waiting limousine yawning open behind. "Violated is such a vile word," letting the syllables linger, "Especially when it's only hearsay."

She offered the crowd the thin, enigmatic smile, of a woman who knew the weight of secrets, and the cost of their keeping.

Other voices clamored, each question rising and falling in the twilight, but she was already gone, the heavy door closing with a hush that seemed to swallow the noise.

Inside, the world was leather and silence, tinted glass and the faint perfume of power. Wells drove.

Outside, the steps glowed in the last light, and the city held its breath, waiting for the next answer, the next secret, the next move.

TWENTY

The oval and the edge

THE OVAL OFFICE was quiet, but not still. President Hamilton sat beneath the painted sky of the Resolute ceiling, a cigarette burning between two fingers like a slow fuse. Across from him, Jessica Peake sipped coffee from a White House china cup, her expression unreadable. Behind the couch, a silent male nurse stood like a sentinel. At the far end of the coffee table, Chief of Staff Nicholas Porter leaned forward, his elbows on his knees, eyes flicking between them.

A personal assistant moved with practiced grace, setting down a tray of snacks and pouring coffee. No one thanked her. She didn't expect it.

Hamilton exhaled a plume of smoke, watching it curl toward the ceiling.

"Not a bad idea: a demonstration of your technology. Can you give us one, without blowing up the world I mean?"

A pause. Then, a dry smile. "Gallows humor. Sorry."

Jessica's reply was quiet. "No, that's OK. I deserve it."

Porter offered a conciliatory nod. "Nice pivot with the Senate Science Subcommittee, by the way. And don't take it too personally. They have a gift for rubbing people the wrong way."

Jessica didn't blink. "The line of questioning was legitimate. So was my answer. I could spend days explaining my technology and they still wouldn't understand."

Hamilton stubbed out his cigarette in the ashtray at his side, leaned forward, his voice low and urgent. "So, let's help them. Make it simple. But make a statement. We need something to get the taste of that other thing out of our mouths."

Porter stood and began pacing, a habit born of long hours and a restless mind. "You know, there's an old abandoned whaler sitting off Portsmouth Harbor. If we could haul it out of dry dock and take it to sea, we could use that for an on-site demo."

Hamilton's eyes lit with mischief. "Good idea! I love the symbolism. Make a show of it: Senate Defense Committee, a couple of Joint Chiefs. Set up a viewing station on the bridge of the USS *Harry S. Truman*."

Porter blinked. "An aircraft carrier?"

Hamilton, bursting at the seams, said, "Abso-frigging-lutely. Make it a party. Flyover from the carrier deck. Set it up somewhere in Dr. Peake's part of the world. Off the southeast corner of the Bermuda Triangle."

Jessica raised an eyebrow. "It's hurricane season. I'll need at least three months to set it up and test it."

Hamilton's grin was wolfish. "Parkinson's Law. Now or never. You've got thirty days. Work expands to fill the time available for its completion." Smiling across at Jessica. "You of course know that."

He turned to Porter. "Coordinate it with Doug Mallory."

Porter hesitated. "Sir? Vice President Mallory? Is that the best way to go?"

Hamilton's voice dropped, almost tender. "Given my current situation, it has to be. He is my legs...for now."

Jessica's tone shifted. "Mr. President, about VP Mallory... Could we talk...in private?"

Hamilton glanced at Porter, who nodded and rose. As he passed Jessica, he murmured, "Thank you." She acknowledged him with a silent nod.

Hamilton gestured to his nurse, who helped him into his wheelchair. Once he was seated, the nurse exited quietly. The President wheeled himself behind his desk, the motion slow but deliberate.

"Jessica," he said, settling in, "I know what you're going to say. I've known Doug Mallory for thirty-five years. And he doesn't really want my job. He only acts like he does."

Jessica, knowing full well Mallory's intentions, joined him, coffee in hand. "I think you underestimate his ambition."

Hamilton shook his head. "Oh no, I don't. But frankly, I'm running out of options."

She studied him. "Sir, how are you... really?"

He turned toward the window, gazing out at the Rose Garden, where the light was beginning to shift. "Not good. A fragment of the bullet that lodged in my spine is still there. And if they try to remove it, I have a 90% chance of becoming quadriplegic." He turned back, eyes hard with the truth.

"If I leave the fragment in, it could seep into my system. I hit complete sepsis within 24 hours. And it's game over. So, either way, I'm a ticking time bomb."

Jessica's voice was barely above a whisper. "How many people know?"

"Right now, only my nurse, my doctors and me. But that's for now." He paused. "Just get me a winner, will you? Do the demo. And work with Mallory to get it."

She nodded. "You have my word."

Hamilton grinned. "Done. And don't worry about the $1.5 billion. I can hide that much in my underwear."

Jessica smiled and placed her coffee cup on the desk, then walked around and took hold of both Hamilton's hands. "I will be thinking of you, I really cherish our friendship, thank you."

Jessica stepped onto the gravel path in the White house front drive just as Vice President Doug Mallory approached from the opposite direction. They met and faced each other on the lawn, the air between them taut with mutual distrust.

Mallory smiled without warmth. "Looks like we're joined at the hip. Try not to fuck it up."

Jessica didn't blink. "I'll try to resist the temptation."

She walked away from him leaving Mallory standing with an arrogant, self-assured grin, almost a smirk, on his face.

Jessica slipped gracefully into the rear of her limousine. Wells closed the door behind her with practiced care, leaned in to murmur instructions to the driver, and watched as the vehicle glided smoothly into the flow of traffic. As the limo disappeared around the corner, Wells turned and strode toward two waiting agents. Without a word, they climbed into their own car and followed at a discreet distance, their presence almost invisible—shadows trailing in Jessica's wake.

Mallory put his iPhone to his ear, speaking into it as he turned his back and walked towards a waiting black limousine. His voice was low. The recipient unknown.

TWENTY-ONE

What's happening?

IT WAS A NEVADA SUNRISE. A lone desert highway stretched out, endless and empty, its silence broken only by the distant hum of a dark blue truck with Air Force insignia catching the first pink rays of morning. Already, the heat shimmered above the asphalt. It had been over 90 degrees through the night, hinting at the promise of the day's relentless burn.

Josh Green, who was in his late thirties, stepped from the cab, boots crunching on gravel outside an old, battered roadside diner. He was dressed in blue, sun-faded fatigues hung against his frame, the kind worn by men who kept watch in the loneliest posts on earth. Over them, he wore his leather flight jacket, the creases of a thousand dawns and midnights evident, and the small insignia of his trade: Nuclear and Missile Operations, showed dull beneath the dust marking him as one of the quiet brotherhood of missilemen, guardians of a silence too vast to speak of.

He paused, taking in the hush. Nothing but the echo of his own breath and the faint, far-off call of a morning bird, most likely a roadrunner skimming across the desert floor could be heard. That sound, quick and fleeting, only made the stillness more intense.

For a moment he stood there, a man shaped by endless underground hours where clocks ticked slow and screens blinked with the weight of worlds, now facing nothing more dangerous than the sun-baked door of his local desert diner. Yet the habit of vigilance clung to him, and his eyes swept the horizon the way a soldier checks a launch key twice.

Inside, the diner was a time capsule: chrome and vinyl, walls crowded with black-and-white photos of pilots and planes. The air was thick with the scent of coffee and fried bacon, the soft drone of a television played news in the background.

Silver-haired Albert stood behind the counter. He looked up with a half-smile. "Morning, Josh."

Josh grunted, slumping onto a stool, elbows planted on the counter as if bracing against the world. Albert slid a newspaper his way and poured him a coffee dark as midnight. "Usual, josh?"

Josh cracked the paper open, eyes scanning headlines. "Al, have I ever asked you for anything else in how many years?"

Albert chuckled, voice rough with memory. "Too many. Just being social, Josh. It's a beautiful morning, if you haven't noticed."

Josh just grunted again, the sunrise lost on him. He flicked the paper open, the headline blaring:

CLOSED SENATE HEARING: WHAT'S HAPPENING?

A grainy photo of Dr. Jessica Peake, storming down marble steps, glared up at him.

"She's Doctor Who, Einstein and Oppenheimer combined, this one is," Josh muttered, jaw tightening. "Who in hell does she think she is?"

He jabbed a finger at the newsprint, voice rising. "You read this crap, Al?"

Albert shrugged, unbothered. "Yep. And if you ask me, she's on schedule, that one. Always is."

Josh's voice sharpened. "Yeah? On whose schedule? Who knows who's paying the bitch under the table."

Albert returned with a plate full of scrambled eggs bleeding ketchup, bacon curling at the edges, toast and hash browns crowned with green chiles. Josh didn't thank him, just stabbed a chile, stuffed it in his mouth and swallowed it with a bitter swig of coffee.

From a booth by the window, a man watched, eyes heavy with worry. Josh caught the stare and bristled. "What? What you looking at?"

The man shook his head, voice soft. "Nothin', Josh. It's just… well, I think it's gettin' to ya. Down in your bunker, you and that button."

Josh raised his right index finger, trembling with anger. "I have more power in this finger than Doctor-fucking-Einstein-Peake!"

He stabbed at his eggs, causing yolk to splatter across his face. Albert offered him a towel and Josh snatched it, wiping his face with the roughness of old wounds.

He shoved the plate away, newspaper tumbling to the floor. With deliberate spite, he ground his heel into Peake's face, the newsprint crumpling beneath his boot.

Albert stood there, about to pour Josh another coffee. "Finish ya breakfast, Josh."

Josh strode out the door, slamming it so hard it cracked the glass—a jagged fracture in the morning calm.

Albert just shook his head and turned back to the flickering TV. He flipped through the static until he found an old movie. Elvis was singing, somewhere between heartbreak and hope: "I'm all shook up."

Outside, the desert waited, empty and endless, as the day began again.

TWENTY-TWO

The middle of the riddle

THE LATE AFTERNOON SUN dipped low over Boston, casting dappled shadows through the trees across the Charles River. Autumn had arrived in full regalia, trees ablaze in fiery reds and golds, their leaves drifting in quiet legions to the ground like forgotten prayers.

Jessica Peake strolled arm-in-arm with her old mentor, Sir Anthony Wood, along the weathered stone footbridge. He was nearly eighty-four now, and reduced to leaning heavily on a cane, yet he still carried the air of a man who had once commanded rooms and rewritten the laws of physics.

They paused midway across the bridge, gazing down at a lone sculler slicing through the water beneath them. The oars dipped and rose with practiced grace, the wake a delicate V trailing behind.

"Look familiar?" Sir Anthony asked, his voice warm with memory. "Your glory days for the Crimson?"

Jessica smiled, though it was tinged with melancholy. "Seems like another lifetime. I've lost a stroke or two."

They stepped off the bridge and onto the jogging path, where the crunch of leaves underfoot mingled with the rustle of wind. Sir Anthony winced slightly, shifting his weight onto the cane. "Speaking of losing a stroke," he muttered, "the years have not been kind. Such a bore, this waltz with mortality."

Jessica looped her arm more firmly beneath his. "Lean on me, then. It's the least I can do."

She rested her head lightly on his shoulder. For a moment, time folded in on itself, past and present held in a fragile, golden stillness.

"So why the visit?" he asked. "Surely you didn't fly all the way up to Boston just for a stroll down memory lane."

"Maybe I did," she said softly. "Maybe I needed a safe haven. People of my own house."

Sir Anthony chuckled. "And am I of your house?"

"Of it?" she asked, incredulous. "My God, you helped build it."

"Oh, quit sucking up," he said, nudging her playfully. They both laughed, the sound echoing off the river's edge.

Behind them, a vintage Bentley crept along at a respectful distance. Inside, Sir Anthony's longtime chauffeur, Atkins, kept a watchful eye on the pair. He drove slowly, matching their pace, the vehicle almost reverent in its silence.

Ahead, on another footbridge, a photographer and his model staged a whimsical photoshoot. The model wore an elaborate 1890s dress and twirled a lace parasol. The photographer snapped photos with artistic flair, angling his camera like a conductor leading a symphony of light.

Sir Anthony gestured toward the landscape with his cane. "I love this time of year. Like a Turner painting. You can almost catch the bouquet of the seasons as they lift off the canvas."

"Autumn in particular," Jessica murmured. "God's paintbrush."

"And what about your paintbrush, my young apprentice?" he asked, eyes narrowing with mischief. "Looks like you went pure Hieronymus Bosch on us. That vanishing village had your imprint all over it."

Jessica's smile faded. "It was never supposed to happen that way. An unexpected energy spike blew everything apart. Now I'm doing serious damage control."

"But control, you must," he said. "That's the whole game. Tricky little buggers, those neutrinos. So tiny to pack such a wallop."

"I followed your advice," she said. "Created my own mythology. And now I've unleashed a second Pandora's Box upon the world, complete with all its plagues."

He turned to her, eyes bright. "Ah, but what's the last thing that flew out of that box?"

She sighed. "Hope."

"Exactly. Your main challenge right now is that you're in the middle of the riddle, Jessica. Remember what I told you: there's nothing more dangerous than scientific research that actually creates an outcome."

She looked away. "The curse of my practical nature."

"Perhaps you've been too clever," he said. "You had the right ingredients in the right proportions. But you forgot one thing... You weren't holding the cocktail shaker." Pointing to the sky, he added, "It was."

"But I am now," she said, her voice trembling. "It revealed itself like the Holy Grail. I virtually have my hands on the answer."

"Then shake it," he said, eyes alight. "Shake the bastard."

She stopped walking. "I don't know if I have it in me, Tony. I'm scared."

He turned to face her fully, cupping her face in his hands. "Of course, you are. So am I. So are we all. Fly into the face of your fear, my dear. It's what you've always done. Jessica Peake, you're a bloody modern-day Galileo. If only I'd had the courage to pursue such a revelation. Embrace it. Fulfill your destiny."

From the footbridge, the photographer and model had ceased their posing. The parasol snapped open again: but this time, it was no prop. In a blink, it transformed into a carbine rifle. The camera, disassembled and reassembled in seconds, became a silenced MCX. The photographer and model were no longer artists. They were assassins.

Gunfire erupted.

Sir Anthony's body jerked violently as three bullets tore through his back and out his chest. He pitched forward, collapsing on top of Jessica, shielding her with his body. She screamed, but he whispered into her ear, blood in his throat.

"Stay still. Don't move. Still, shhh... shhh..."

The hitmen advanced, still firing. In the Bentley, Atkins drew his pistol and returned fire before he was struck and dropped, gravely wounded.

Then, tires screeched. A black SUV skidded to a halt behind the Bentley. Jason Wells and another agent leapt out, weapons drawn. Their shots were swift, deadly. The photographer fell instantly, riddled with bullets. The model vanished beneath the bridge, slipping through the metal grids like a ghost.

Jessica clutched Sir Anthony's body, his blood soaking through her coat. She knew the medics would arrive too late.

He looked up at her, eyes dimming. "It's OK," he whispered. "Just promise me... you'll finish what you started."

"I promise," she sobbed. "I promise!"

A strange peace settled across his face. He exhaled one final time and was gone. Jessica let out a sound that was half scream, half moan—raw and primal. Jason Wells approached, but she shooed him away.

"Get away! *Get the fuck away!*"

He urgently spoke into his phone. "Clean up and Medivac... À0-71: Level 4: 3 players, 2 critical."

Within minutes medics rushed in, lifting Jessica gently. One injected her with a tranquilizer and her limbs went slack, and she collapsed. She was quickly loaded into a waiting limo and Wells joined her there.

Rain fell in steady sheets as the limo rolled through the night. Jessica curled into the corner of the backseat, her face pressed against the cold glass. Raindrops raced each other down the windowpane, mirroring the tears on her cheeks.

Across from her sat Jason Wells, who had been silent for most of the ride.

"Where are we going?" she asked, turning to face Wells.

"A secure location," he replied. "You're not out of the woods yet."

"You have a gift for articulating the obvious," she said, her voice hollow.

"I'm sorry for your loss," he offered. "I can only imagine."

"No, you can't," she snapped. "Don't even try."

She turned back to the window, eyes vacant. Outside, the world blurred in streaks of water and light. Inside her, the riddle remained. But now, so did the promise.

She was sad and weighted down by the pain of loss. How deep he was there within her heart. Her guide—her mentor.

She turned back to Wells and said "I must try to have a state of tranquility and freedom from distress and worry." That said, she went back to staring out the window.

As the vehicle passes through the shadow of the autumn oaks, Jessica found herself in a state of serene calmness and contemplative thought. Her quiet resistance to chaos drew inspiration from the writings of Marcus Aurelius, particularly *Meditations,* where the internal world is portrayed as a sanctuary from external disorder. Her thoughts echoed an inward turning, suggesting that peace is not the absence of conflict, but the presence of clarity.

As they pass a large lake, the imagery of still water and open sky becomes a metaphor for the irenic self—the peaceful self—who chooses understanding over reaction, and presence over judgment.

The truth is rarely pure and never simple—Oscar Wilde

TWENTY-THREE

The cold geometry of trust

To be trusted is a greater compliment than to be loved.
—George MacDonald

THE SECRET SERVICE INTELLIGENCE HQ hummed with quiet intensity. Outside, it was a dark night and two armed security agents stood in the shadows.

Inside, screens pulsed with data, the soft glow of surveillance, painting Jessica's face in alternating hues of blue and white. She sat still, composed, but the exhaustion behind her eyes betrayed her. The events at the Charles River had left their mark and it was more than skin deep.

Wells stood beside her, hands clasped behind his back, his expression unreadable. With a flick of his wrist, he summoned a holograph from the panel before them. Twin faces rose into the air, frozen, translucent, and spectral. The two hitmen. Neutralized.

One image lingered longer than the other: the man they called the Photographer.

"They were both Guoanbu," Wells said, his voice as measured as the room around them. "And it was definitely you they were after. We terminated him this afternoon."

Jessica didn't react. She had learned to absorb shocks without flinching. A second image appeared, this time, a woman. Her features were sharp, her eyes cold and distant, even in digital suspension.

"She is still active," Wells continued. "And Chinese Asia puts all its black ops on a do-or-die trajectory. She *will* find you."

Jessica turned her head slightly, her voice dry. "Why are you telling me this?"

"Because you need to know the risk levels. There will be others."

She gave him a wry half-smile. She was tired and bitter. "Nice to know I'm in such high demand."

"They're downplaying your role in today's tragedy," he said. "The narrative will be that the hit was on Sir Anthony, a martyr, silenced for his protests. You'll be scrubbed from the scene."

Jessica blinked slowly. "That's cold."

"I'm in a cold business."

A door opened softly to the side. A young woman entered, plain, androgynous, efficient. She held a small electronic device in one hand, and a needle in the other.

"This is Ms. Krashen from contact tracing," Wells said.

Ms. Krashen's voice was clinical. "Please hold out your arm."

Jessica hesitated, her eyes narrowing as she looked back at Wells. "What is this, *The old Hunger Games*?"

Wells didn't blink. "Yes, and I'm trying to make sure the odds are ever in your favor. This way I'll be able to track you if things go sideways."

"I thought you were here to prevent all that." She extended her arm anyway. Resignation, not consent. The needle slid into her forearm with a sterile pinch.

"It's all breakable," Wells said. "There are limits. You need to be aware. And vigilant. And you need to distance yourself from anyone you might bring into danger. Any loved ones. Your friend Mark Richards, perhaps?"

Jessica stood, rubbing her arm. The chair creaked softly behind her. "I have a plane to catch."

"It's your plane," Wells replied.

"It is," she said, walking toward the door. "And you're not invited."

"I know. But I'll be along very shortly. Like it or not."

He followed Jessica out of the room, down a long, low lit corridor towards the entrance. The two security agents moved from the shadows as Wells opened the rear door of the limo for Jessica, and like a cop placing an arrestee into a police car, Wells placed his hand gently on her head. "In you go." Then he got in and sat beside her.

She was surprised when he handed her the green leather Bisonte briefcase she thought she'd lost. The two agents got into the front seats, and the limo sped away.

When the government limo pulled up to the edge of the private air strip, the Learjet waited like a silver arrow beneath the runway lights, engines humming low and ready. Jessica, holding her briefcase, stepped out into the night. The air was cool, indifferent. She walked without looking back until she reached the foot of the stairs. Then she turned.

Wells was still standing by the limo, the door now closed behind him.

"I've been a bitch," she said, her voice quiet.

Wells nodded once. "You've been through a lot. I understand. You don't have to love me. Just trust me."

She held his gaze for a breath, then nodded. A silent agreement. No promises. Just recognition.

Then she turned and ascended the stairs, her silhouette dissolving into the cabin light. One more figure in motion, caught between danger and destiny, trust and survival, where emotion is a liability and survival is the only constant.

In the shadows and on the shores

THE SUN ROSE OVER the bright Caribbean Sea as Jessica Peake's Learjet descended gracefully onto the island's airstrip, landing on the island of St. Ives. The rhythmic pulse of reggae music floated over the coral waters and the sound of crashing waves blended with the voice of a local island DJ.

"Wake up, St. Ives, St. George, St. Kitts, and all you other lucky citizens in listening range of Radio Caribe!" the DJ's voice crackled through the speakers. "It's Saturday at 7 a.m., and life is waiting!"

Two small fishing boats hauled in their morning catch as eight boys played cricket on the beach. Jessica, behind the wheel of her Wrangler, drove along the sandy road and up the hill toward a small, weathered cottage nestled on the hillside. Mark's cottage.

The reggae faded, replaced by the voice of a polished British announcer.

"We have a terrific slate of great island rock music for you shortly," said the DJ, now affecting a British accent. "But first, some global news from the BBC."

Mark Richards stood at the kitchen counter in shorts and a tropical shirt, slicing fruit. The kitchen opened up to a view of the beach, where the sea shimmered in the morning sun. At the table, Lori munched on a bowl of cereal and fruit.

The BBC news anchor's voice came through the radio, somber and clear.

"Tragedy struck in the U.S. city of Boston yesterday when Nobel Laureate and peace advocate Sir Anthony Wood was shot to death near Charles River Park in what is being described as a terrorist attack. The assassins appear to have been Chinese Asians, but China has denied all responsibility."

The news continued in the background as the doorbell rang.

Mark looked up and walked to the front door. Without looking to see who it was, he opened the door and froze. Jessica stood there, fragile and trembling, her eyes brimming with tears.

"Aren't you on the wrong island?" he asked gently.

"I sure hope not," Jessica replied, her voice cracking. "Mark, I... I can't... I—"

"I know," he said softly. "I heard. God, I'm—"

Sobbing, Jessica collapsed into his arms. "Oh God, Mark! It was terrible!"

"I know it must have been," he whispered, holding her tightly. "I loved him too. I'm so sorry."

From the kitchen, Lori heard the voices and came running, squealing with delight. "Jessica!! I've missed you!" Jessica felt Lori wrap her small arms around her legs. She dropped to her knees and hugged the little girl fiercely.

"Are you back, Jess!? Are you coming to the beach with us?" Lori asked, beaming. She looked up at Mark. "Daddy, can Jess come to the beach?"

Mark looked down at Jessica, who still clung to Lori.

"Yes, sweetheart," he said, "she can if she wants to. But that's up to her."

Later that morning Mark and Jessica strolled slowly along the dunes of a small sandy beach, watching Lori a few yards ahead as she built sandcastles with a group of local children.

"It was my fault, you know," Jessica said quietly. "When they shot Sir Anthony, they were coming for me. God, I feel so responsible."

"You shouldn't," Mark replied. "If it was China, they'd kill everyone just for good measure. Let's face it, the world's a pretty fucked-up place these days."

"Yes," Jessica said bitterly, "it has been like that for a long, long time. How did it get that way? Jesus, Mark. It's our garden, and we continue to destroy it." Her voice trembled. "All I've ever wanted to do is help put the pieces back together. And yet here I am 'Shiva, the Destroyer of Worlds,' just as Sir Anthony warned me."

"Don't be so hard on yourself. I overreacted to that holograph, and I didn't give you a chance to tell your side of the story."

"That's just it. I didn't let you in on my side of the story. I didn't even try. I've always had trust issues with hidden agendas."

"Jesus, Jess. You *are* a hidden agenda. You're the most secretive person I've ever known," Mark said with a wry smile. "And I'm the guy who's in love with you. That little girl over there and I," he gestured toward Lori, who was laughing with the other children "we're your biggest supporters."

Jessica leaned into him, wrapping her arms around his waist. "I know," she said softly. "And you two are the reason I came. But it turns out I'm a danger to both of you. People may try to harm you to get to me and I can't let that happen."

"I can deal with it," Mark said. "But when they threaten my little girl…Look, Jess, it's not like I don't know what you're up to. I mean, using neutrinos for particle disintegration and reformation that's the science of the future."

"No," she said, her voice firm. "It's now. And I've decided I need you to help me with it. Now."

"Are you serious?"

"Mark, you've known me for twenty years. I'm always serious."

She looked up at the sky, then back at him. "The reason I came here this morning was to tell you that I was a danger to you and Lori, that I couldn't see you until this blows over. But that's the wrong path."

She stopped walking and turned to face him. "The truth is I need you, Mark, to help me with my work. Don't get me wrong, Taylor is the best. He's a rock star. But right now, I'm this close," she held her fingers a breath apart, "to finding the missing piece. I've got a one-time demo coming up in February, and I need all the brainpower I can get. So..."

Mark stared at her, stunned. "You mean you're offering me a job?"

"Well, I guess so. I mean, if you're in danger, the safest place for you and Lori is with me. And you can help me with my work." She smiled. "God knows there's a bit of a learning curve."

"Maybe not as much as you think," he replied. "Why do you think I took my Master's in Quantum Physics in the first place? I wanted to someday maybe work with you again. Like we did before you quantum-leapt away from us all after MIT."

"Mark," she whispered, "I've loved you my whole life. But you know that."

"I know." She nestled into his arms, and they embraced. But then Jessica's eyes caught something down the beach.

"Who's that with Lori?" she asked, pointing.

Mark followed her gaze. A woman, attractive, unfamiliar was talking to Lori. Her presence was wrong—too poised, too perfect. She reached out to Lori with a smile that didn't reach her eyes. The moment passed but for Jessica there was a chill—her enemies were no longer shadows. As soon as she noticed Jessica and Mark approaching, the woman turned and quickly walked away down the beach, then began to run.

They ran to Lori. "Lori, honey, who was that?" Mark asked, kneeling beside her.

"Oh, a very pretty lady with a funny accent," Lori replied innocently. "She asked me if I wanted to come away with her. But I guess she changed her mind."

This attempt by the unknown woman was chilling, especially in contrast to the idyllic setting. Was it a signal to Jessica that enemies were closing in?

Jessica looked directly at Mark "I'm the target,"

From a rocky outcrop above the beach, Kamila Dimitriova, a New Soviet agent, peered through binoculars. Standing beside her was a tall, burly operative named Panke Yassov. *Does their surveillance suggest a broader international conspiracy, Obviously tied to Jessica's technology?*

Through the lenses, they watch Jessica, Mark, and Lori, framed perfectly in their crosshairs.

Wells, with his long lens and Parabolic microphone, captured it all, as his thoughts cataloged the scene: *A family in fragile reunion. Spies on foreign sand. A child nearly taken.*

The brief but tantalizing mention of "using neutrinos for particle disintegration and reformation" implies a level of speculative science bordering on quantum teleportation or molecular reconstruction. It positions Jessica's work as both revolutionary and dangerously coveted. Other nations would be like a wolf pack hunting her and sniffing her down until they can eat their prey. But I'll be here in the shadows, her safety.

TWENTY-FIVE

Ghosts in the code

IN A QUIET CORNER of a windswept coffee shop in St. Ives, Agent Jason Wells nursed a cooling mug and a growing obsession. His laptop glowed with the cold light of classified firewalls, each one more stubborn than the last. He leaned in, fingers tapping with the rhythm of a man used to secrets.

On screen was a photo and name: Mark David Richards. A red stamp reading "Top Secret Access Denied" was slashed across the photo.

Wells frowned. "Well now," he muttered, voice low and edged, "all you're doing is pissing me off." He typed again. And again. Fingers flying in a symphony of code, frustration, and relentless intent.

Then—click.

"Got you," he whispered, eyes widening. "Son of a bitch."

The files opened like a flower. Folder after folder, a dark trail of data unraveled before him. The shadowed journey of a man who had once vanished into the folds of government secrecy. Wells stared, then buried his face in his hands.

"Holy shit! Why has this never been mentioned?"

He shut the laptop with a snap and slid it into a black case. He placed a few bills on the chipped saucer, slung his shoulder bag across his frame, took one last bite of the egg and bacon sandwich and then he was gone out the door into the misty afternoon, carrying with him the weight of revelation.

Jessica Peake's villa

The world felt warmer at the villa. Mark and Lori arrived in a dusty leased Mini Cooper, welcomed by the scent of salt air and the laughter of home. Maggie appeared first, arms wide, and Lori leapt into them like a bird returning to a familiar nest.

"Well now," Maggie cooed, "won't we all have a lovely time?"

Jessica smiled, her eyes catching Mark's. "Won't we just?"

Later, Jessica led Mark through the heart of her hidden world, her Atlantis. The control chamber was always a cathedral of light and data for Mark, where holographic galaxies spun in midair and neutrino fields shimmered like living auroras.

"Here it is," she said, her voice reverent, "the universe in which we shall now play."

Mark's eyes revealed a great depth of gratitude and love. "I love the math of it. Always have. So precise."

Jessica tilted her head. "Yes and no. That's the danger. It's not just numbers anymore. It's alive. Breathing. Volatile."

The images danced across their faces: stars, oceans, particles, maps. Jessica's voice softened, turning almost poetic. "I remember what Einstein said," she continued. "I read it in a book called *Conversations with Einstein,* back in 2023. 'The neutrino is like a fish in the universal ocean. Its molecular structure becomes a screen through which consciousness flows.'"

Mark nodded slowly. "So they become as one."

"But that's just the starting point," she said. "And thus, begins the paradox."

Her phone buzzed, slicing through the moment. She glanced at the screen and saw *Jason Wells*. With a flick of her thumb, she silenced it and tucked it away.

Days blurred into nights. Jessica and Mark immersed themselves in the work—holographs, equations, maps of unseen forces. Lori and Maggie bonded in the sunlit corners of the villa, building fantasy houses and sharing secrets. Taylor joined the inner circle, bringing his sharp mind and sharper tongue.

Inside Atlantis, data swirled like a storm. Jessica, Mark, and Taylor moved like dancers between glowing panels, chasing the elusive patterns of the universe. They scribbled notes, argued over energy permutations, and high-fived over small victories. It was a rhythm of obsession, of discovery.

At last, trusting Mark Jessica took him to the Skywalk above the Neutrino Collection Chamber. Beneath them, the chamber pulsed with silent power, an ocean of subatomic ghosts.

She walked it first, unafraid. Mark followed, reassured by her steadiness.

He was more than impressed, he was astounded by what was revealed to him.

Deep in the heart of the command center, Jessica had fallen asleep on her favorite couch. Mark, still awake, draped a blanket over her and returned to the glowing data. His fingers moved with purpose, eyes locked on the shifting holograms.

Behind him, Taylor had silently entered, walking quietly, observing Mark.

"Ease up," Taylor said. "You can't absorb all this in a few days."

"I'm gaining on it," Mark replied without looking up.

Taylor smirked. "Mostly, it's gaining on you."

Mark turned. "That's the beauty of physics. It's all math. Once the algorithms are in place, the rest falls like dominoes."

"That simple, huh? Aren't you the genius. You do realize that we are completely locked into the Collection Chamber?"

"I'd already guessed that. You don't like me, do you?"

"I don't know you," Taylor said, leaning on the table. "But I think you're ambitious…and dangerous. Mainly because you think you know more than you do."

"The only way to grow," Mark said, "is to reach just beyond your grasp."

Taylor laughed, sharp and skeptical. "This is more than reaching. We've spent years chasing one ghost particle. And now you think you're the Ghostbuster who's going to 'complete the canvas'?"

Mark met his gaze. "Maybe I am."

"Jessica Peake is like Picasso, remember him?" Taylor snapped. "Her colors are beyond anything you can imagine. And you think you're going to 'complete' the canvas? Shit, man. You crack me up, Mark."

He turned, noticing Jessica fast asleep on the couch and decided to leave. He chuckled to himself and said, "Do *not* press the wrong button."

On the couch, Jessica stirred beneath the blanket. She opened one eye, then closed it again. Her phone buzzed once more. She glanced at it and saw it was Wells again. Agitated, she let it go to voicemail and drifted back to sleep. She was ready, Hamilton's request was ready, it was all set.

TWENTY-SIX

Whale of a surprise

DAWN BROKE OVER THE Caribbean Sea. The ocean, restless and churning, whispered secrets beneath the wind as it skimmed the surface, following a rusted anchor chain as it climbed toward the belly of a forgotten old behemoth: a whale factory ship, now still.

She sat like a ghost upon the waves, tethered not to land, but to something far stranger, a floating continent of refuse, a plastic island born of human carelessness. Her hull, once white with salt and spray, was now just rust and memory.

A launch approached, cutting through the morning breeze. The old captain of the whaler, unshaven, weathered and solemn, stepped aboard the deck with the second mate close behind. Three technicians, who were bent over intricate machinery, looked up as he arrived.

"All in place?" the captain asked, his voice gravel over the calm.

"Yes, sir," replied the first technician. "Just as Dr. Peake and Admiral Johnston specified. We're just setting down the last pair of highly intricate transmitters."

Sophisticated sensing devices sat secured on the afterdeck. The captain gave a nod, and at his silent command, the crew began to debark.

The captain took a radio phone from a senior crewman as the launch, now slicing away into the waves took them away from the ship. He stared back at it, once his ship those many years ago now, as it grew smaller in the distance.

"Launch to Showboat," he said. "Moby Dick is anchored, cleared and ready." He lingered a moment longer, eyes on the fading silhouette. "End of an era," he murmured.

Above, the sky answered with the chopping rhythm of rotor blades.

The helicopter, a sleek HMX-1 Nighthawk, call sign *Marine 2*, hovered like a dragonfly over the waterlogged leviathan. Inside, Vice President Douglas Mallory and Senators Woodbine and Polisky peered down at the derelict ship and its strange companion: the swirling, colorful mass of plastic waste.

Mallory's gaze was hard and calculating as he made a simple gesture to the pilot, who tilted the chopper away from the ghostly vessel.

"Showboat, this is Marine 2," the pilot called. "Request clearance to approach."

"Marine 2," came the reply, "auxiliary deck is cleared for your arrival."

The U.S.S. *Harry S. Truman* loomed ahead, a fortress of steel and might. The helicopter settled on its helipad as the blades slowed to a sigh. The door opened and a platform lowered.

Mallory stepped down, flanked by the senators and Secretary of the Navy, Alex Ritt. They were met by Admiral Marcus Johnston and his executive officer, Commander Swift. Salutes were exchanged, and pleasantries passed like currency. The Secret Service hovered nearby, ever watchful.

From the bridge, the crew observed Vice President Mallory in silent anticipation as he walked beside Admiral Johnston.

"Are we ready to start the show?" Mallory asked.

Johnston checked his watch. "Yes, sir. Just as soon as Dr. Peake gives the word. Thirty-four minutes and counting."

Commander Swift stood before a wall of screens, his fingers dancing across controls. "Magic Maid, this is Showboat," he said into the comm. "We are locked and loaded. Synchronizing our times. 31:30:29."

Far away in Atlantis Control Center, Jessica sat at her station, flanked by Mark and John Taylor. Her voice came through, clear and sure. "Showboat, this is Magic Maid. We are locked in. On my cue. Over."

Back on the bridge, Admiral Johnston led the VIPs to the viewing deck. Mallory, ever the showman, muttered under his breath. "Please, God, no fuck-ups this time."

He turned to the senators. "If this is what we think it is, every nation on Earth will soon have a stamp on its ass that says 'Property of the United States.'"

Johnston, overhearing, looked around to Senator Woodbine with a knowing nod of his head. "Game change?" he asked.

Mallory grinned. "Game over."

He slapped the admiral on the shoulder as they reached the glass-walled deck. Johnston checked his watch again. "Still over thirty minutes. I would suggest—"

"A drink?" Mallory interrupted. "Good idea. Something stronger than coffee?"

Senator Woodbine chuckled. "At this hour, I need all the help I can get."

Commander Swift motioned to a young lieutenant JG, who stood at attention. "If you'll follow Lieutenant Dominico to the Viewing Bridge, they can get you anything you like."

Mallory's eyes lingered a moment too long on the young officer's retreating form.

The senators and secretary followed. Admiral Johnston watched them go, his expression tight. "There he is, ladies and gentlemen," he said quietly to his XO. "Vice President Douglas Mallory. Just a heartbeat away from POTUS."

TWENTY-SEVEN

The birds have flown

THERE WAS A HAZE of tension aboard the *Harry S. Truman,* it's viewing bridge already stirring with activity. Two Secret Service agents flanked the entrance, as a young ensign, barely more than a teenager, offered Bloody Mary's and steaming coffee to the gathered big wigs. The air was thick with anticipation.

Far from the ceremonial calm, Jessica stood at the helm of her control center, briefing Taylor and Mark with tight urgency. "We've got one chance to get this right," she declared. "Let's just hope those little monsters behave themselves this time."

Taylor, ever the realist, offered a sliver of optimism. "This time we have more pieces in place."

Mark raised an eyebrow. "You mean, you've had pieces missing before? Talk about gun slinging."

Taylor smirked. "No people this time. Just a ghost ship anchored to an island of plastic the size of New Jersey."

"Plastic?" Mark echoed.

"Yeah," Taylor replied. "Ninety percent of all 'recyclable' plastic isn't. It ends up here—about ten million tons of it." He paused, "The worst thing that humanity ever invented."

Watching Mark's expression shift, he asked, "Well now, Mark, are we losing our virginity?"

Jessica cut in. "We're twenty-seven minutes to countdown. I need someone on the thrusters at the Neutrino Hangar and the Propagator. They're preset, but I want an onsite failsafe."

"I can handle it," Mark volunteered.

"No," she said firmly. "Too much to go wrong. And too much pressure on you. Stay here with me, Mark."

Taylor grabbed his gear and took off, double checking the screens as he left.

A black Suburban rolled to a stop at the security gate. Agent Jason Wells stepped out, folder in hand and introduced himself to the sergeant at the gate, who on giving Wells an inquisitive glance, radioed-in his arrival. "Agent Jason Wells for you. Says it's classified."

Jessica's voice crackled through the speaker. "Good God, not now! Tell him to leave it and come back tonight after six."

Wells shook his head. "She *has* to know this," he said, shaking the folder in the air. He got back into the Suburban, reversed up the drive, turned and, tire's spinning, sped away.

Down in control center, Jessica muttered to herself, "Jesus. Talk about timing."

On the bridge of the *Harry S. Truman,* Vice President Mallory sipped his drink, surrounded by senators and staff. Below, Admiral Johnston issued the order: "Magic Maid, we're eleven minutes and counting. Release the birds in one minute."

The flight commander's voice came over the intercom. "Aye-aye, sir. 00.55.00:50."

The flight deck roared to life. The afterburners of the first re-designed F-35 11 fighter burned white hot as it set to launch. Flagged by the deck officer, it burned into what's rapidly becoming a dark, cloudy sky. It is followed by a second, third and fourth F-35, ripping from the flight deck into the darkening sky.

On the bridge, Commander Swift leaned toward Mallory and said, "Big Dog wanted a flyover, sir. So, you're getting one. Blue Angels. Second generation."

Mallory beamed. "Outstanding."

Back at Jessica's control center, she reacted to what she has just seen on the screen. She runs over to the control panel area and pages Admiral Johnston. The news hits like a slap.

"Birds? What birds? Showboat, get back to me!" she demanded.

Admiral Johnston's voice came through, calm but final. "Big Dog specifically ordered a flyover."

"No flyover! That was the deal! Reel them back in! Over!"

"Sorry, Magic Maid. The deed is done. The birds have flown. Out."

Jessica, in frustration, takes hold of a water glass and hurls it across the room "Shit!! *Shit!!*"

Mark jumps up. "What?!"

Jessica switched screens, replacing Taylor's face on one of the screens with a quad display: the whaler, the aircraft carrier, Taylor in the Neutrino Hangar and the Central Neutrino Collector area. The images shift with her strokes.

The Neutrino Collector Globe began to glow, beams of light pulsing through its core. Taylor notes the activity level as he examines various monitors. He sees that the Neutrino levels are already red-lining. Reading maximum intake. He touches the intercom section of one of the screens freaking out. "Jesus! We're already maxing out! The center will not hold!"

"Hang tough, John. There's another level to this."

In desperation he shouts, "Now you tell me?" Taylor continues to shake his head in disbelief.

Jessica remotely stabilizes the Collection Chamber and, for a moment, equilibrium returns. It has settled it back into safe parameters.

On the Bridge of the *Harry S. Truman,* Mallory, the Senators, Admiral Johnson and several senior officers watch expectantly on a large screen as the molecular structure of the Whaler starts to break down.

Mallory more than excited shouts, "It's showtime, folks!"

Cheers erupt, though Admiral Johnston and his staff remain stoic.

Back in the Neutrino Hangar Collection Chamber the Neutrino Propagator surged with light and heat, its energy red-lining. On the register, it accelerated from vibrant to violent. Taylor, continued to fight to dampen the controls, but the system refused to yield. Now it was a sign of a propulsion of matter already red-lining. Unnerved by the velocity of the increase, he tried to tamp down several valves. Unsuccessful, he backs away.

Taylor, now more than anxious, shouts "Hey Jess, we're hitting critical mass! Can you override?!"

Back at Jessica's control panel the control keys refuse to respond — and the launch is in a matter of minutes. "Fuuuuuuuuuk! John, we're frozen here! All the keys are locked!"

"Here too! The breakers won't move!" Taylor yells, now in distress.

"Hang on, John, I'm on my way. On second thought, open the Propagator." As she slips away from the console she grabs a jacket and runs up the stairs, fixing one of her shoes as she runs." Bugger!"

Mark calls to her, "I'll take com—"

Jessica cuts him off, shouts "Mark, just stick to the codes I gave you."

She calls Maggie. "Maggie, I'm gone for a while, take care of Lori. Sorry. Give her anything she wants. You know what I mean."

The wind slammed the door behind her as she dashed to her Range Rover She opened the gates with a touch on the dash, and speeds toward the hangar.

The section of the Neutrino hangar roof opens and the arm of the Neutrino Propagator rises and begins to open like a mechanical lotus. It becomes luminous, with petals of light unfolding and vibrating erratically as it emerges from its protective silo and locks into place.

Jessica, now inside the Hanger, practically flies across the gantries. She notices a few of the emergency lights flicking on and off as she joins Taylor at the controls. He is struggling as he reads the data screen: Energy transport to Geo Coordinates: Lat 26.5 Long 76.89 K.M.L. 108.50.

Jessica placed a hand on Taylors shoulder, commenting, "The particle storm has begun. John, why isn't the screen on? Turn it on!"

Instantly they see the whaler floating under a dark, stormy sky. Light waves begin to fracture the ship's molecular structure, and its particle energy begins to disappear as it becomes a glow of white light in the turbulent ocean waters. It is haloed by a translucent, circular, moving cloud. They both see clearly that the Neutrino bombardment on the whaler's deck is beginning to work. It looks as if it's vaporizing the whaler.

The plastic island to which it was tethered vanished instantly, as if ripped up by some gigantic invisible hand. Energy waves surge aft in towering waves of light toward the open sea and the carrier five nautical miles away.

Aboard the *Harry S. Truman,* Admiral Johnston and Mallory stand as the rays of light reach them. The bow of the carrier begins to dematerialize in shafts of light. F-35 Lightning Jets streak above the carrier and within seconds their molecular structure fractures into thousands of particles of light. They vanish mid-flight.

"What in God's name is she bringing down?" Mallory shouts. "This is a shit show!"

Jessica and Taylor flicker, literally, as their bodies began to phase in and out. "It's like they're controlling us!" Taylor gasped. "Mark, clue us in! What's happening over there?!"

An astonished Mark's voice comes over the com. "Everything's breaking up at the source. We're frozen! None of our fail-safes are working!"

Panic erupted on the carrier deck and crewmen scattered, some vanishing into thin air, only to reappear seconds later ahead of the disintegrating launch platform, the prow of which dissolved before their eyes.

Admiral Johnston and the Staff Officer, having witnessed in horror the dematerialization of the prow section of their carrier, are completely freaked out as a trio of seamen jump overboard to escape, but they vanish instead, only to partially re-compose on the way down.

Admiral Johnston is in a mental state of panic but tries to contain himself. "My God, we could all vaporize!"

Mallory, the senators and the crew fight to leave the bridge and do a runner towards the rear of the Carrier, and see the prow and landing deck vanish completely before their eyes. Everything within a 200-degree span of view is phasing in and out on the way to disintegrating.

The Hangar

A thunderous sound seems to encircle the entire chamber. Jessica looks down at her body mass as it starts to break apart, staring at her disintegrating hands. She shouts to Taylor over the deafening sound, "I've got to get inside the chamber and hope to God I hit the right keys from there! When I get inside, count to twenty. If I don't come out, pull the thrusters! It's our only shot!"

Taylor, concerned for her safety, says, "Boss don't! It's a crapshoot! It's an unknown!"

"I'll just do it! And let's hope to God I'm able to pull it off!" Jessica said as she raced up the chamber ramp. She coded the door with her palm and disappeared inside.

She dashed across the override platform, her breath sharp, her purpose unshakable. She touched the keypad and entered her sanctuary of science and faith. Fading now, her form flickers, but her hands remain steady. She engages three large buttons with a reverent touch, eyes closed in a silent invocation. Her fingers press the three thrusters within the Neutrino Collector, particulate energy stirs and a cosmic ballet ignites. The chamber swells with Neutrinos, a universe unto itself, replete with trillions of tiny stars that take on mass and form. They congeal slowly, majestically—an embryonic universe born in containment.

Jessica is stunned by what she is witnessing happen to her physical body—cell by cell she is dematerializing, and she begins to dissolve. It's a pixelated disintegration. Her body surrenders to the field, her very essence merging within the unseen Universe.

Taylor, at the controls outside of the Neutrino collector, counts down with grim precision. At twenty, he slams the keys, initiating a counterpoint—a harmonic disruption to the building energy. The chamber reacts. Walls shimmer. Air fractures. His body flashes, disassembled and instantly restructured.

In the Atlantis area, Mark and the entire control center vanish. Then in a sweeping surge of cellular reassembly they reform, whole again, as if nothing happened. Yet everything has changed consciously.

Maggie, in her cottage, holds Lori tightly, somewhat stunned by the same experience. Softly and with surprise, she says, "Lori, that was a magical wonderland, wasn't it? Shall we do that again?"

Admiral Johnston, now alone on the Bridge, watches as the bow of the aircraft carrier dissolves into nothingness, then reforms as if undergoing a hyper-speed rapid reconstruction. Every bolt and beam is returned.

An F-35 fighter materializes mid-landing, and three more follow. The flight crew reappears on the deck as it also rematerializes. All seems to have returned to normal…But it is a new normal.

Jessica is suspended in the Neutrino field in the Capture Chamber. She is there…and not. Her form splits, fractals of her being caught in the storm. She becomes a shower of glistening white light. Her mouth hangs open, maybe in fear, maybe in disbelief, maybe in horror. There is one loud scream and she is gone. The area is empty, a silent void.

Dark skies brood above where the rusty factory ship once was, along with the island of plastic that housed thousands of countless shoals of fish and turtles. Now gone.

Under the same darkening sky, sitting in a small fishing boat, Elena Dimitriova and her Russian film crew have captured it all. The cameraman hands her a micro disk. She uploads it to a laptop, her fingers trembling slightly. History, saved in silent frames.

Mark steadies himself having experienced his entire body and the control center turn into particles of pulsating light and then re appear. He sits with both hands on the console and notifies Taylor, "We're back at zero gravity here. Mission accomplished! What a trip! Are you okay? How's Jessica?"

On the grid, Taylor scrambles down to the Capture Chamber. He places his palm on the scanner and the door slides open. He enters, then stops, gob smacked by what he sees: An immense field of trillions of Neutrino particles, swirling and suspended replicating what appears to be a tiny universe. Alive. Expanding. But of Jessica, there's not a trace.

His own body immediately begins to become surrounded by radiant light. Without any hesitation he leaves the Chamber. Jessica has disappeared, and it is a turning point for him emotionally. His reaction is layered and deeply human. He's visibly shaken, though he tries to suppress it.

He experiences a physical stillness, almost like a pause in his entire being, which contrasts sharply with the chaos around him. It's as if the disappearance pulls the rug out from under his carefully balanced worldview. Internally, he experiences a mix of fear, even guilt, and self-doubt. *Wait doubt about what? What she has created? What she cannot control?* Jessica was not just a colleague but also a symbol of the hope and trust he'd placed in her Irenic process. Her disappearance feels like a personal failure.

"Did I miss the signs?" he screams. *Did my commitment to diplomacy blind me to the real threats of the hidden power of the Neutrinos?*

Until this point, he has been unwavering in his belief that dialogue can solve everything. But now, he can see the first cracks in that belief. He starts questioning whether idealism alone is enough when the stakes become personal.

In short, his reaction is a blend of emotional vulnerability and evolving conviction. Is this feeling to mark the beginning of a more complex, perhaps more pragmatic version of John Taylor. "Where is she?" He shouts echo through the chamber. "Jessica, where are you?"

Wells parked his Jeep in the circular drive of the villa and has managed to persuade the guard to let him through. That accomplished, he pulls up directly behind the parked Wrangler as Maggie, Lori and Mark appear on the front terrace, their faces filled with question upon question.

Taylor steps up towards them. "She's gone. I don't know where. She just disappeared!"

Maggie's hands go to her temples. "Oh God, Jessica! John, what happened?"

Wells is now standing one step below, behind Taylor. "Gone? As in vanished?"

Mark picks up Lori, and with his free arm around Maggie's shoulders, says, "What do you mean, vanished?"

TWENTY-EIGHT

Eternal essence

A LOW GROWL ECHOES in the darkness. Torchlight flickers against stone and earth, casting crooked shadows as it arches toward a skinny dog barking into an open, rubbish-filled ditch

"Get away, you filthy mutt!" snapped an old man's guttural voice.

The dog yelps and scurries off. The man, holding a burning torch, steps cautiously toward the ditch. He lowers the light, revealing a body lying face down in the filth. Slowly, he turns the figure towards him. He calls out in shock and surprise as he steps back He looks again, more closely and in Hindi shouts, "It's a woman!"

The formerly unconscious, her body slumped against a dried dirt wall, stirs. Her limbs tremble with shock and she's filled with disbelief. Her eyes fluttered open, then shut again, struggling to focus. "Where... am I?" she whispered weakly.

She tries to rise, but her strength fails and she collapses back against the wall.

From an open doorway, the curious, weathered faces of septuagenarian mountain villagers and children of various ages peer at her. An old, wrinkled woman stepped forward, kneeling beside Jessica with a metal pail of water and a rag. She dipped the cloth in the water and began to gently wipe Jessica's face and hands.

"Rest, child. Rest now," the woman said in Hindi.

A young Punjabi girl came to Jessica's other side, lifting a gourd of fresh water to her lips. Jessica drank greedily, then looked around, her mind slipping into surrender. Her eyes closed and in a fraction of a second, she was gone. Gone back—or forward—into something beyond.

High in the mountains above Patna, India, the mist hung like a drifting cloud through moss-covered woodland. At first light, the village roosters crowed, and a middle-aged villager waved down an old army Jeep rattling along a narrow dirt trail.

The Jeep slid to a halt. A sergeant and two Punjabi soldiers jumped out, pushing through the crowd of villagers who blocked a small hut's entrance.

"Clear a path! Now!" the sergeant barked in broken English.

Inside, Jessica stirred. Her eyes opened as the soldiers shoved aside the old woman and young girl who had cared for her. The sergeant loomed over her. "Documents, please?" he snapped.

"American... I'm American... U...S...A..." Jessica mumbled.

The soldiers yanked her to her feet, but she collapsed. They dragged her, feet trailing in the dirt, through the crowd. The villagers shouted in protest. Children of all sizes following them. The soldiers zip-tied her wrists and shoved her into the barred rear cabin of a battered Mercedes police van and slammed the doors shut.

The old woman stood in her doorway, holding a bowl. Others joined her, watching in silence as the van pulled away. The old woman cryptically said, "Don't you men dare hurt her, the gods will not be happy with you if you do."

Washington, D.C. Dusk. Number One Observatory Circle.
Douglas Mallory stood on the Vice President's balcony, a coded smartphone pressed to his ear. "Missing? What do you mean, Jessica Peake is missing?"

Mark Richards is standing on the circular drive close to one side of the villa, with a backup iPhone to his ear. "Mallory, I mean she's disappeared. Disintegrated, for all I know!"

Mallory gripped the railing. "In which case we're fucked. No Jessica Peake, no secret weapon."

"On the contrary," Mark said coolly. "She left me with all the algorithms and the codes. I can replicate her formulas. She's virtually redundant."

"Jesus," Mallory muttered. "I thought I was callous."

Mark glanced up and noticed Maggie peering through a window, so he moved further onto the side terraced garden.

"Casualties of war," he said. "The point is, I've got this. It's mine now."

"Give a monkey a Stradivarius," Mallory snapped sarcastically.

"The Consortium will feel differently when they hear it from me," Mark said as he walked through the terrace towards the ocean and sat on a stone bench.

Mallory's patience snapped. "The U.S. military gets the technology first! That was the deal, Mark. You do understand that, don't you?"

Mark leaned down and picked up a stone. "This is a new deal," he said coldly. "New rules." He indignantly pitched the stone into the ocean.

In anger Mallory responded. "You turncoat little shit! I'm doing my job! Are you?!"

Mark moved from the terrace back into the lounge. "Are you threatening me?! You fucking pygmy?!" Mark again picked up another stone and this time just threw it aimlessly into the sky.

Mallory slammed his hand into a vase of flowers that crashed down on to the stone fireplace hearth. "Shit, that hurt. Let's end this conversation."

"I don't threaten," Mark said. "The Consortium does it for me. They own your ass. And mine." He walked back through a side door into Jessica's lounge and right into Maggie. He immediately backed out and closed the door behind him.

Silence. Mallory had hung up.

Mark stared at the phone. "We both know it," he whispered, He tucked the phone into his trouser pocket and entered the villa. He walked back into the lounge and there was Maggie dusting the mantle.

Mark, somewhat embarrassed lied. "I'm sorry, Maggie I was on the phone with one of Jessica's old friends who wanted to know where she was. I said that I didn't know. It was a difficult conversation."

Maggie knew what was going on, since Wells had briefly mentioned something to her. "It's quite all right, Mark. Lori is sleeping. Why don't you go and see if she is okay?"

Outskirts of Patna, India

At midday the old prison looms, its filthy, weathered clay and stone walls towering behind ancient wooden gates. Crowds fill the dirt street and press between dilapidated shops and crumbling buildings.

Scott Mitchell, a thirty-five-year-old sweaty AP reporter in a stained camera vest, gnawed at a Vada Pav as a Mercedes van screeched to a halt. A sergeant in a Jeep followed close behind.

Two soldiers opened the van doors to reveal Jessica, looking mangled, disheveled and dazed. The soldiers dragged her toward the gate. One driver slammed the back doors shut.

Mitchell's eyes widened. He dropped his food and pushed through the crowd. "Jessica Peake? Dr. Peake? It can't be!"

He reached the sergeant. "Dr. Peake? Is that you?"

Jessica looked up, barely able to see. "Where... am I? Where the fuck am I? Help me..." Mitchell raised his camera and snapped a few shots before the sergeant shoved him against the prison doors.

"All right. Okay. You break this and you pay for it" Mitchell muttered, pointing to his camera and backing off.

The sergeant gave him a look that communicated he'd rather kill this foreigner than look at him. Mitchell managed a few more photos as Jessica was dragged inside. A guard noticed, cursed him in Hindi, and Mitchell melted into the crowd.

Once they had taken her through the gates, the soldiers dumped Jessica in the dirt courtyard. Two guards approached, lifting her more gently and escorting her through a metal door.

They passed packed cells filled with ragged, reeking men who catcalled and jeered, making crude remarks. One guard unlocked a rusted gate and led her into the women's section. Inside, the stench was unbearable. A woman defecated in the corner, while others who were bruised, veiled in surgical masks and crawling with lice, watched her. The guard shoved Jessica into a cell and locked the door behind her.

Timid hands reached out, pawing and patting her. Jessica stood frozen, unsure what these poor women would do to her. Wondering if she would be respected or torn apart. She summoned what little Hindi she knew and said, "We're all sisters here. Sisters, are we not? Where am I?"

Later that afternoon in downtown Patna, Mitchell wove through the chaos of the city, dealing with broken sidewalks, cluttered alleyways and sweat-streaked crowds until he reached a faded sign reading: *Patna News*.

Inside, it was a cacophony of ceiling fans, smartphones, and knock-off computers. A throwback of the 2020s. Mitchell dropped into a chair, wiping his phone with a stained handkerchief. On the floor next to his chair, a young boy was pulling a rope attached to a Punkahwallah ceiling fan that wafted a breeze above Mitchell's head.

"All right, all right, calm down," he said into the phone. "Now, repeat it back: Jessica Peake is in a really disgusting old prison not too far from Patna." He listened, fidgeting.

"Jesus H. Christ! How the hell should I know? But she's here in Pa—"

A screech came through the phone. He pulled it away from his ear.

"Just get it off to the wire services. ASAP. Thank you!"

Through a small window, Jessica felt a cool breeze that was drifting down from the Himalayas. She sat crumpled in a corner, away from the cesspit, though the stench still lingered. Her head rested on her knees.

She thought of Ab Barik. The same event that devastated that village had happened to her. That meant the others, those who'd vanished, might still be alive.

She recalled the Neutrino Dome Chamber, where matter and energy blurred, where identity dissolved. *Was that moment science or transcendence? Did my dissolution into the neutrino field symbolized humanity's merger with the cosmos? A sacrifice for a new paradigm?*

She breathed deeply. *The whaler's and the air craft carrier's reassembly, their disappearance and return, the crew, the natural order, it all points to something greater. Something timeless.*

Her eyes tried to focus in the darkness as thought after thought swirled through her mind. *The uncontrolled power of so small a molecule. I am part of Creation? It is Creation trying to know itself? Am I Creation trying to know myself? I can only infer the essence. Nothingness? The space between. It is the space between everything?*

She whispered phrase by phrase. "Tired. So tired. The science of life? Eternal peace?" With even a softer whisper. "How?" She closed her eyes.

"I must sleep. Try to sleep. Divinity? Is that how they disembody?

"Masters of their eternal essence. Shit," she muttered. "It stinks — And the noise." Oblivion.

TWENTY-NINE

Profound science is wonder

PRESIDENT HAMILTON SAT UPRIGHT in the expansive hush of the presidential residence, propped against a mound of pillows. Morning light filtered through the tall windows.

"Do you know who Einstein was? Quite a brilliant man. 'The most beautiful thing we can experience is the mysterious. It is the source of all true art and science.' Einstein said that." Hamilton looked across the room to a figure standing there, a silhouette against the window light.

Mallory. He stood there, summoned and steeled, like a nervous soldier awaiting orders. Hamilton waved a printout from the AP wire bearing the quote, his voice sharp with disbelief even though he's frail. "It's a famous statement from the past, Mallory! We got the super weapon demo of a lifetime. But our girl vanished and turned up in Patna, India. How in fuck-all Mother Mary and Joseph did that happen? Science and the mysterious, Mallory!"

Mallory remains composed, though the edges of his fatigue show. "I can't be in so many places at once. I certainly can't control this woman's technology and science. Apparently, neither can she!"

Is Mallory hinting at the limitations of intelligence and surveillance in the face of transformative, possibly a metaphysical, phenom-

ena? Hamilton wondered. He's also very aware that the Consortium are showing their exhaustion in trying to manage events beyond their comprehension.

Hamilton's tone hardens, but his eyes betray something deeper: a flicker of fear. "What we *can* control is who finds out about it. Get to our embassy in New Delhi and get her out of there before the wheels come off."

Mallory nods and turns to leave. "I'll return with her. I am out of here, sir."

Patna, India

Two days later, in a dim hotel bar, Mitchell sits hunched over a drink, talking to two old, sozzled English pensioners, regaling them with tales of espionage and scandal. Behind him, Agent Wells enters, quiet but purposeful.

"Well," Mitchell slurs, "Every shithole has a silver lining. Once my story breaks, I'll be going home in style."

Wells steps up beside him. "Mitchell?"

Mitchell turns to see who has just mentioned his name, and Wells continues. "I'm sorry to let you know that we've had to table your article... for the moment."

"You've what?" Mitchell says, incredulous. "*By what authority?"

Wells' hand dives into a pocket and he flashes his credentials, "The President of the United States."

Mitchell scoffs and tries to stand, but stumbles as he does, pulling out his phone and jabbing at the screen. Wells reaches to steady him.

"She's here rotting away as a guest of the Patna Constabulary. You'd know that if you saw my story, which is probably down some bureaucratic rabbit hole by now."

Wells doesn't flinch. "Don't worry. You'll still get your scoop. And your fee. Just not yet."

Mitchel, even with his drunken boasting and personal ambition is overtaken by the national security concerns.

He steps away, pulls out a secure phone, and makes a call. "This is Agent Jason Wells, Division PAC 37 Number 461709. I have Priority One clearance for the release of a United States citizen, Dr. Jessica Peake."

In the grimy prison cell, Jessica sits cross-legged among a group of women, reverently focused. Somehow, she has shifted the energy of the space from filth and despair to calm and quiet. Although they can hear the noise from the men's area—cursing, shouting, making intense obscene calls to the women—their calm is not disturbed.

When the guards arrive, they hesitate, somewhat awed by the transformation and shocked that not one of the women screamed at them. With unexpected gentleness, one guard unlocks the gate and both move toward Jessica, lifting her to her feet. Leaving, she nods and smiles to the women and in Hindi says, "Thank you for your kind friendship." Jessica had experienced a deepening sensitive cultural connection with the women in the cell around her.

As she's led down the corridor, the oppressed women who had found some hope in this transcendent person who had only spent a short time with them began to chant, "Jessica! Jessica! Jessica!"

Jessica blinked against the blinding sunlight as she's guided to a battered Land Rover. "Late as usual," she murmurs upon seeing Wells.

Wells approaches the captain of the guard, handing over official papers, and acknowledging answering her snide remark as he does. "You're kind of hard to keep track of, Dr. Peake. Turning to the guard, he adds, "These are for the release of Dr. Jessica Peake. I am now responsible for her safe delivery to the American Embassy in Delhi."

His Sikh driver translates for the captain of the guard, who give a subdued salute. The younger guard releases Jessica, and she stumbles, finding it hard to stand without support.

Seeing this, Wells' face is etched with concern. He allows Jessica to lean against him and puts an arm around her to keep her from collapsing. The driver comes around to help, and they both gently support her and help her into the backseat.

Wells climbs in and sits beside her, making certain that her head is comfortably cradled by his backpack. As they start to drive away, she sits up, looks back at the prison and shudders. Wells offers her a flask of water, she takes a long drink and falls back into the backpack.

The Land Rover winds through the local countryside, passing small villages and fields where farmers plough the land with their long-horned oxen.

Time passes and eventually Jessica is awake and staring out the window, completely in her own conscious space. Wells, silently observing her, leans behind the rear seat and retrieves a small canvas bag filled with some personal belongings and hands it to her.

In a sympathetic tone, he says, "Since I haven't quite mastered the finer points of intra-terrestrial travel, we're taking a train to the Embassy in New Delhi."

Jessica turns from the window, shakes her head, and says, "Can I get cleaned up first?"

"We have a room at the Lemon Tree hotel. We'll be there in about an hour."

Jessica points beyond the driver… "No. There. Now, please."

Through the windshield, a rock formation appears with a waterfall cascading into a crystal clear, serene, pool. The area is devoid of people.

"Tamil, stop here," Wells instructs the Sikh driver.

As the Land Rover pulls over, Jessica wipes her eyes, takes the bag, and steps out. Wells watches her, then hands her two white garments that weren't in the bag.

"A spiritual anomaly," he mutters to himself. "Well, why not? Mine is not to reason why."

"Thank you," she says, looking back up at him.

Wells gets out of the vehicle and helps her to walk slowly through a grove of trees and down to the water's edge. He leaves her there beside the water and then sits quietly in the dappled shade.

Jessica dips her bare feet into the water, turns, and takes a quick look at Wells before she strips and steps naked into waist-deep into the pool. She takes the crystal-clear water into her cupped hands and throws it onto her face, handful after handful. Each splash of water brings her a feeling that the neutrino light, ethereal and protective, and unseen is the force guiding her transformation.

She wades closer to the waterfall and submerges herself beneath it. Rising, and letting the waters cascade over her, she turns 'round and 'round, ecstatic. It was an emotional release for her.

Wells looks briefly, discreetly, at her naked beauty before she again submerges. When she rises in the middle of the pool, sunlight streams through the canopy, illuminating her like a benediction. She lifts her face skyward, and with a deep internal longing she calls softly to the sky in a moment of surrender and openness for a divine guidance, "I feel so lost. Help me... please? Please help my heart understand." She raises her arms skyward and continues, "Let me know and understand if there is a mission for me here on Earth. What is my purpose?"

She lowers her arms, swims away from the waterfall and then under. There, with eyes open, she feels as if the water is bathing her with love. The clear waters of the pool now are her comfort.

She rises, her wet hair clinging to her face. As she pulls it away, she sees a woman across the way. She's maybe in her early forties, and she's with a young boy, maybe her son. They begin to wash clothes in the shallows.

The boy looks up, smiling warmly, and Jessica drops down into the water to cover her nakedness. She stares in shock; he is the exact image of the boy from Ab Barik. The boy who disappeared. He smiles with a look of warmth and kindness.

Jessica turns and swims to the edge of the pool, then rises and gets out. She then takes the long white shirt Wells had given her and puts it on, all the while staring at the young boy.

The woman gathers their things and approaches carefully across various stepping stones. She unwraps a blue batik scarf and offers it to Jessica. In a soft-spoken voice with an Indian accent, she says, "You are no longer lost. Every cell of your body knows this. That which creates life, you are, and that which is life, you are. You are One."

Jessica hesitates, but then slowly takes the scarf, draping it over her head and shoulders. Silence moves gently between them as Jessica reflects on what the woman has just said.

"My name is Jessica. You speak English? Did you hear my prayer?" Jessica asks as the boy lets go of the woman's hand.

"I do," the woman replies. "I speak many languages. I am Mala. And this scarf is a gift for you."

"Mala," Jessica repeats the name softly, knowing the meaning is illusion.

Mala smiles. "Jessica, Mahatma!"

Jessica gazes down at the scarf. Celestial patterns shimmer across its surface, as if lit from within.

"'Great soul? Mahatma?" she questions. "I am hardly worthy of this remarkable scarf, Mala."

"Oh, but you are." She gestures to the scarf that Jessica now holds in both her hands. "You are now aligned with a greater universal purpose, Jessica."

Jessica's eyes become radiant as she notices patterns come alive within the scarf, as if shot through by a billion celestial bodies. Jessica is in awe, opening up the scarf as she observes a cosmic show unfolding before her.

Mala takes Jessica's hands in hers and they hold the scarf together. "My gift to you is already part of you. You carry a burden that weighs you down with guilt. Know that In India we call it Maya, illusion. All that is lost will return to you as it was. Intact."

Jessica fights back her tears. "I've been scattered like sands in the wind knowing that I have the power to destroy, but not create."

Mala's voice is steady. "Yet here you are: a Pisces soul at one with the ocean of inspiration. Allow the healing to come through every cell in your being. Be willing to receive those moment-by-moment messengers. Listen to your silent voice and flow with the matrix of Creation."

Jessica's voice is barely a whisper. "Is that which I have experienced God? Is there a God?"

Mala's rhetorical response reframes the question. "Is there a Universe? Is there a Primal force of Creation?"

Rather than a personal deity, she invokes a universal creative principal—echoing pantheistic where all is divine. God is identical with the cosmos.

Without warning, she leans in and kisses Jessica in a tender, sensual way, charged with something ancient and unspoken, an emotional intimacy.

Mala continues. "The Great Principle stands forth as a Golden Light. It is not remote. It is within all of us. Hold yourself inside its glow and you will behold all things clearly. For when your doors of perception are cleansed everything will appear as it is, infinite," Mala says as she lets go of her hands.

Wells, who has been listening to all that has been said, stands as he's taken by the feeling that Mala's discourse has given him.

Jessica breathes deeply. "So, when the doors of perception are cleansed, life will appear as it really is? Infinite... And yet, as a scientist, inexplicable."

Mala embraces her once more, then takes the boy's hand. As they turn to leave, Jessica calls out. "He's such a beautiful boy. What is his name?"

"Asha," Mala replies. "Asha, meaning Hope.'"

Taken by the meaning, Jessica's tears begin to fall again.

As they walk away, Asha turns back with an innocent, knowing smile.

He's the same boy…the same eyes. Jessica thinks as she drops to the edge of a rock, trembling. *Could he really be the very boy from the village at Ab Barik?* Her tears continue to flow and she begins to sob, as she wraps the scarf tightly around herself unfolding its moving celestial patterns with her heart.

THIRTY

The Rajdhani Express

PATNA JUNCTION TRAIN STATION heaves with life, an ocean of color and movement. Families and wanderers converge in a dance of castes, sects, and customs. Everywhere there are camels loaded down with baskets, tied-up goats, and crates of chickens. The station pulses with heat and humanity, a living mosaic of saris, turbans, and the scent of spice and sweat.

Amid the chaos, Jessica moves like a ghost in white, her top and pants stark against the kaleidoscope of Indian color. Beside her, Wells scans the crowd, ever vigilant.

As Wells pushes aside a young man carrying a large, tied carpet bundle on his head, he takes Jessica's hand and climbs up into the

Rajdhani Express. He jumps with surprise as it exhales hot steam through his legs.

The crowd surges, elbows and voices raised. People are dragging bundles and bleating goats, while children clinging to mothers, and elders try to cling to dignity. Women with their children scramble and push their way onto the train, while others climb up onto the roofs of the carriages. The second-class cars are a crush of desperation.

Jessica watches as a mother with two children battles for the final seats, only to be shoved aside by men twice her size. She retreats to the floor, her dignity intact but bruised.

Wells mutters, "Trust me, I did try for a chopper."

Jessica doesn't flinch. "It doesn't matter."

They push forward toward First Class. Two men in *Pagari* head-dresses, tall, dark, and saturnine, watch Jessica with unsettling hunger, their *katar daggers* glinting in their belts. Wells clears the path, shielding her from their gaze. She brushes past them, her spine straight, her silence louder than fear.

Inside First Class, the contrast is jarring. Ornate woodwork, velvet seats, and polished brass, exude a slight opulence that mocks the chaos outside. Their compartment, 24A, is a capsule of stillness.

Wells breaks it. "For what it's worth, you really made it happen back at St. George. You disintegrated the whaler, along with the island of plastic the size of Rwanda. All without a single casualty."

Wells makes certain that the door is closed and ensures that Jessica sits by the window, facing the direction the train will travel. He then sits opposite her. Jessica looks around, concerned and making certain they are safe.

"Except for me," Jessica's voice is a whisper. "I just want to get back to the people I care about, Mark and Lori, and my work."

Wells hesitates, agonizing over what must come next. The weight of the information he carries regarding Mark weighs on him. He takes a folder from his backpack sitting by his side on the well-worn seat.

"There's no good time for this," he says, handing her a folder marked Classified.

Jessica takes it as if it might burn her. She focuses on the word Classified, staring into space before opening it.

"I wish it could be otherwise," Wells murmurs, then slips from the compartment as Jessica opens the folder, noting the "CIA/DO" designation on the leaf.

She opens it slowly, hesitantly. Not certain what will be revealed. *Why did he leave?* She wonders as she pulls out the first sheet. On it is Mark's face, familiar, smiling, and now suspect. She reads the damning words that accompany the photo:

Political Operative

Double Agent

China

The New Soviet Union

Jessica's breath catches. Photos cascade like betrayals. Mark with young Mallory at a college fraternity party after the Yale vs. Harvard match. In another photo she recognizes a group that includes Mark and the American Oligarch from the Consortium, dated Spring 2027. Another shows Mark with foreign agents, appearing to meet with a Chinese operative, circa 2029.

Tension, frustration, sadness and dire agony war within her. Her heartbreak is not just personal, it's existential. It becomes her. She throws the contents of the folder to the floor, and one sheet lands almost in slow motion, with Mark's face looking directly up at her.

She falls back into her seat, the train's rhythm mocking her.

The journey continues, refusing to acknowledge her inner turmoil. Outside the windows, towns and villages blur, a virtual mural of beauty in the midst of dire poverty. At every stop, she sees the faces of the people and phase into visions of lost loved ones from her life. Each face a ghost. Moments stolen. And the flicker of Mark's smile.

Her memories betray her. Beach days with Lori, the warmth of Mark's hand, the fire of their love, the passion of their purpose. All of it, now in question.

Glancing once more out the window, she glimpses a mother and small boy standing on a platform. The woman and boy both have tears streaming down their faces. Jessica blinks. *It's Mala. Or is it?* She bolts upright and turns as the door opens to reveal Wells standing there.

"I'm sorry," he says.

"No! No, you're not!" she screams. "You're not! Why show me this now?" She picks up the empty folder and throws it at him. It hits his face with the weight of her heartbreak. "You insensitive asshole! I hate your fucking guts!"

She storms out past the elegance of First Class, down the corridor, and into the press of humanity in Second Class. She's on her way to the rear of the train, stumbling over and through women with children and bundles of luggage in the aisles. Her tears are raw and visible, her pain a beacon. Some of the passengers fall silent, watching her pass like a wounded angel.

She storms onto the caboose balcony, dust and wind lashing her face. A furious torrent of invectives rips from her lips, scattering into the twilight—a raw, piercing cry that shatters the evening's silence. "God damn you, Mark! God damn you for making me love you and put my faith in you! God help me! Who can I trust?! Who in God's name can I trust?!" Her voice cracks, echoing into the darkening expanse beyond the rails. The words hang in the air, raw and trembling.

She exhales a shuddering, broken gasp, and with it, the sharp edge of her anguish seems to loosen its grip. Her hands clutch the cold iron of the balcony as if it's the only thing tethering her to the world. For a moment, she bows her head, letting the wind whip through her hair, the ache in her chest throbbing with every mile the train carries her away from the life she thought she knew.

As she leans forward, she is suddenly bombarded by a myriad of shimmering particles of light. They swirl around her, impossibly vivid, encircling her in a halo of consciousness. Disbelieving, she buries her face in her hands, but the particles persist, glimmering, ethereal, their presence both alien and comforting.

Neutrinos, messengers of the unseen, form an invisible, protective shield around her. She doesn't resist. Instead, she surrenders to the phenomenon, letting acceptance wash over her.

When at last she lifts her head, she finds the same two men wearing their *Pagari* head wear standing in the doorway of the caboose. They don't advance. Instead, as if compelled by what they have just witnessed, they slowly sink to their knees, dazed and reverent. For just as they approached, they too saw the light of the neutrino shower surrounding her and passing directly through her, billions of minute particles every second.

The sight halts them, transforms them. In that instant, the violence is forgotten. For them that moment had become sacred.

Wells, who had seen the two men approaching Jessica as if to do her harm, perhaps even to rape her, arrives, gun drawn. He lowers it as he sees that the danger has gone. What remains is something else entirely. An epiphany has taken place.

THIRTY-ONE

The Knight's Gambit

THE AMERICAN EMBASSY in New Delhi rises like a relic of another empire. An old British Raj manor, its bones echo colonial horrors, greed, ambition and cruel diplomacy. On the second floor, Jessica turns in a slow, deliberate twirl, her new skirt and loose suit jacket catching the filtered light of the interior courtyard below. Jason Wells watches her with a mixture of admiration and concern.

"Quite a transformation," he says, arching a brow. "Prada?"

"Neeta Lulla," Jessica replies, her voice playful but distant as she raises her left shoe heel. "I mean, when in Rome. The Ambassador's wife took me."

"Ah. Fashion therapy." Wells admires her shapely calf and smiles.

They move together down the broad, timeworn wooden staircase, its surface polished smooth by generations of footsteps. The quiet of the corridors enveloped them, disturbed only by the soft click of Jessica's heels on the marble floor. Lost in thought, she glanced at Wells, her voice dropping to a hush. "What should I say when I go in there?" she asks, gesturing to their destination.

He doesn't hesitate. "The truth..." he doesn't finish that thought. "Just go with your instincts."

Two U.S. Marines stand sentinel outside the Ambassador's chambers. They salute as Wells opens the door for Jessica, who nods in gratitude, then steps inside alone.

The room is vast and austere, an opulent chamber dressed in restraint. The black-and-white tiled square floor resembles an over-sized chessboard, and a portrait of President Hamilton presides over an ornate fireplace. A well-worn red leather chair sits to one side. On its right, a large antique mahogany desk rests angled into the corner, and on it, there's a large translucent screen.

Jessica inhales the air of power and memory. Then, a familiar silhouette emerges from the shadows beyond the balcony. "Knight to King Four," Mallory murmurs, stepping forward with theatrical precision. "Check!"

Jessica doesn't flinch.

"You don't look very happy to see me. It doesn't matter," Mallory says. "I'm here at the behest of the President. To bring you home. You are the woman of the hour. Check Mate!" He steps onto the center of a black square closer to her.

"For him, I'll come. Tell him," she sarcastically responds, thinking, *You haven't seen my next move, Mallory.*

"I'll do you one better," he says. "Please turn the screen on and tell him yourself."

She does as he asked, and within seconds the frail image of President Walter Hamilton flickers to life on the screen. Even through the digital haze, his decline is unmistakable. He is clearly fading.

"Jessica Peake, dear friend," he says in a raspy voice. "I even had you tagged, and you still jumped ship on me! Every pun intended."

"Mr. President," she says softly, "we did it."

"Sure as hell did! *You* did, anyway. Get back here, we've got work to do. You disappeared an island of plastic the size of New Jersey! Think of the environmental applications." It is clear that

Hamilton is laboring to speak, even though he is putting on a brave front.

"My kind of guy," she smiles, but her eyes betray the sorrow blooming in her chest.

Hamilton's voice weakens. "Hurry back to us. I need to see you for a whole host of reasons. And be nice to Mallory. I know he's kind of a dick, but he's all we've got."

"Of course, sir. I'll do my best." Even before she finishes, Hamilton signs off and the screen goes dark.

Jessica slumps into the red leather chair, her composure cracking. "Oh God," she whispers, "I knew it was serious, but he's fading so fast. How did he get that way?"

"I wish I knew," Mallory replies.

"Of course, you know," Mark Richards says as he steps into the room, the shadows peeling off him like regret.

Cracking the pregnant pause, he continues, "Douglas Mallory knows everything about everybody, and all the reasons why."

Jessica's breath catches. She rises abruptly from the chair, steadying herself with one hand on the fireplace mantle. Shock ripples through her, leaving her momentarily speechless—she wants to speak, but the words die on her lips. Mallory, watching closely, notes the tension in her posture and the tremor in her voice.

"I wanted this to be a surprise for you," Mallory says dryly. "But it seems that Mr. Richards has surprised us both."

"Mr. Richards surprises no one," Jessica snaps. "Mr. Richards is irrelevant."

Mark stiffens, aware that Wells must have revealed his past to her. "Jessica, I can explain everything."

"What a pathetic cliché," Mallory snaps, quick to attack.

"Jessica, please don't walk away." Mark's voice trembles as Jessica's hand tightens on the mantle, her back rigid, knuckles white.

"I know you saw my dossier," he continues, his words filling the silence. "I know who tapped into my sealed records."

Jessica's shoulders flinch, a barely perceptible shudder running through her. She doesn't turn, but her breath comes faster, uneven.

"But you don't know why." The words hang in the air. Jessica's lips part, as if to speak, but nothing comes out.

"I was seventeen when The Consortium tore my family apart." Mark's confession cracks something in her composure, and she closes her eyes, fighting the sting behind them.

"They blackmailed me into doing unspeakable things, even in college."

Jessica's grip loosens. She finally turns, searching his face, pain and disbelief mingling in her gaze.

"Since then, Jess, I've spent my life trying to turn it back on them. But I never, never let that touch how I felt about you." His voice breaks.

Jessica stands motionless, the weight of his words settling between them as her heart pounds with confusion and something like hope.

Unable to hide her sense of betrayal, she turns and retreats to the balcony overlooking the garden, her back to him.

Mark turns to Mallory. "Give me a minute."

"No, I don't think I will."

Furious but contained, Mark is forced to maneuver around Mallory, who deliberately tries to block his way and says, "Leave her be."

Mark moves quickly out to the balcony to make his plea to Jessica. She keeps her back turned as he reaches her.

He stops, intending to pick his words carefully.

Jessica turns, raising her hand as if to block his presence. "Stop! For God's sake, just stop. You know, Mark, I can always tell when you're lying... because your lips are moving."

She takes a step away, then pauses. "I forgive you. Just know that I forgive you for your intellectual arrogance, your sociopathic ambition, and your willingness to sell out everyone to get to the heart of who you think I am. But hear this: if you ever come near me, my work, or my people again, I'll shoot you myself."

For Jessica, forgiveness is not weakness, it's sovereignty. Her threat is not rage, it's boundary. She is a woman who has learned the cost of truth. In her anger, she pushes him aside and walks back into the Ambassador's chamber. She walks past Mallory and out the door, slamming it behind her.

Wells is quietly waiting for her, and they both disappear down the corridor.

Mallory turns to Mark, his gaze cool, unreadable. The look on his face carrying a sense of smugness and disdain. "Am I to assume you've overplayed your hand? Why am I surprised?"

"You fucking asshole," Mark seethes. "You did this. You dropped the dime on me! You sold me out. I know you're the one."

"And how would I benefit from that?" Mallory smirks.

"In a thousand ways I can think of. You think you've got me? I've got you. And wouldn't the *Washington Post* and *New York Times* love to know what dirty business Douglas Mallory is really up to these days?"

Mallory doesn't flinch, instead he backhands Mark, sending him sprawling. "Try it, and you're a dead man. You are anyway. You're no longer of use to us. You're no longer of use to anyone. You're so fucked."

Mark lunges at Mallory and they crash to the floor, fists flying. Digby Stahl and two other agents dash into the room and pull Mark off Mallory, then slam him to the floor. Stahl keeps him in place with a knee in his back, and says, "You've just assaulted the Vice President of the United States," then presses a pistol to Mark's neck. "Twitch, and I'll put a bullet in your head."

As the agents keep Mark pinned to the floor, Mallory stands back and calmly uses a handkerchief to wipe the blood off his mouth. "Let him go," Mallory says calmly.

The agents hesitate.

"I said, let him go."

The agents give Mallory a questioning stare at his casual response.

"Yes, sir," Stahl says, reluctantly helping Mark up from the floor.

"Damn straight!" Mark shouts, trembling with fury.

Mallory stares Mark down while the agents hold him between them, then says, voice cold as ice, "See Mr. Richards out of the building. Get him out of my sight and take him as far away from here as possible."

Mallory then walks toward the desk, pulls out the chair and sits, as he continues to wipe the blood from his lip.

Mark starts to react, but stays silent, he realizes he's already a ghost.

As the two lesser agents frog-march Mark out of the building, Mallory says to Digby, "Let me make a call. We have a flight to catch. Make certain she and Wells are on it."

Once on the plane, Jessica has made herself comfortable, reclining in her reclined chair. A few minutes after Air Force Two has taken off, she's sound asleep with Wells sitting to her right on the other side of the aisle. The sky outside fades into violet as the plane climbs on its way to Washington.

They had been cruising for approximately forty-five minutes when Wells noticed the sudden stir around Mallory's seat. Georgina Milomett, his assistant, approached quietly, lowering her head to talk. "The President's taken a turn for the worse. There have been...developments."

Wells, hearing this, unbuckles his seatbelt and moves toward Jessica. Touching her shoulder gently, he whispers. "Jessica, wake up."

She stirs. He indicates Mallory and Georgina deep in conversation. She releases her seatbelt and says, "Sorry, I was fast asleep. I'll go and see what they're up to."

As she sees Jessica approaching, Georgina steps aside. Mallory, with no hesitation says, "Jessica, the President is now paralyzed below the neck."

Jessica is visibly shocked.

"He's sinking fast," Mallory continued. "At his request, I'm invoking the 25th Amendment. I'll be assuming the office of President. I just want you to know, this is the last thing I wanted."

Jessica studies his face to see if he's being truthful, and says, "I take you at your word."

As Colonel Martin Kane approaches with a large black satchel, Jessica recognizes it instantly and stands to one side. Wells, in the meantime, has edged closer.

"The Nuclear Football, Unfortunately, part of the job," Mallory responds with self-importance. "Your favorite part, I think."

Jessica walks away, the weight of history pressing against her spine.

The plane lands at Andrews Air Force Base under a pale morning sky. As Mallory debarks he is immediately engulfed in a new entourage of aides and assistants, as media cameras click away.

In the quiet wake, Wells draws Jessica aside and says, "We have a changing of the guard, so I may be reassigned."

"I don't want to lose you," she says as she leans against his shoulder and they walk toward her waiting car, the world shifting beneath their feet.

THIRTY-TWO

The exchange

THE BUILDING IS A SKELETON of its former self, forgotten, gutted, and silent. On the edge of Miami's industrial corridor, the wind rattles broken glass in its frames. Inside, there's only a table, two chairs, and the cold glow of twin laptops.

A lean, nondescript man known only as "The Agent" by the Consortium, sits in complete stillness. His posture is military, but his eyes are unreadable. Behind him, a security officer waits in the shadows, unmoving.

Footsteps echo across the room as Mark Richards enters. His demeanor is calm, almost casual, but his eyes are sharp. In his hand, he carries an object, peculiar and out of place—a pickle jar.

The Agent doesn't blink. "You have the flash drive?"

"I do," Mark replies as he lifts the jar and unscrews the lid. Nestled inside, beneath vinegar and dill, is the flash drive.

Without another word, The Agent swivels one of the laptops toward him. The screen flickers to life, revealing the face of a man known only as the "American Oligarch." His image is crisp, his voice even sharper. "Mark Richards, at last. We have your thirty million. You have the Neutrino Cluster algorithms."

Mark's lips curl into something between a smirk and a warning. "Which you, in turn, will sell to China for at least a billion."

"That's not your concern," the Oligarch replies. "What you need to be concerned with are the consequences should these formulations not be viable."

Mark leans forward slightly. "You've already checked them out, or I wouldn't be sitting here."

The Oligarch gives a nod, then turns his head and says, "Make the transfer."

The screen goes dark and The Agent inserts the flash drive into the second laptop. Code begins to scroll, rows of numbers, sequences, equations. He studies them with the precision of a surgeon. Then, he turns the laptop toward Mark and says, "Enter your password. It must be at least eight characters that includes one letter, one number, one symbol."

Mark types. The screen shifts and a digital counter begins to rise, showing millions of dollars flowing into a numbered offshore account.

He barely has time to exhale before the Chinese Hitwoman steps forward from the shadows. She's the same one from the Charles River incident weeks ago. Her movements are fluid, silent. She raises a silenced 9mm pistol and fires two rounds into Mark's skull. He slumps forward. Dead.

The Agent calmly removes the flash drive from the laptop. He hands the device and the machine to the Hitwoman. Without a word, both of them move into the stairwell. But fate has one more twist to offer. On the lower level of the same abandoned building, the Agent and the Hitwoman prepare to part ways. They exchange no words—just a nod.

Suddenly two muffled shots erupt from the darkness, and they both drop to the floor, dead.

Digby Stahl emerges from the shadows and walks with purpose, stepping over the bodies without pause. He picks up the laptop, pockets the flash drive, and disappears into the night.

It's early morning. The studio lights of MSNBC are soft, but the expression on Brian Williams' face is anything but as he delivers stunning news to the world:

"Breaking News: We interrupt this newscast with a special announcement. Walter Hamilton, 49th President of the United States, is dead."

He pauses, allowing the weight of the words to detonate like a bomb. *"The President experienced complications from sepsis that led to toxic shock in the early hours this morning."*

The world has just changed again.

THIRTY-THREE

Peace, like power, is always leveraged

MORNING ARRIVED LIKE A HUSH over the island, the Caribbean sun rising slow and golden above the sea's edge. Its light touched the high palms first, then the whitewashed walls of Jessica Peake's villa, and finally the helipad, where the wind from an approaching Cobra helicopter whips the fronds into a frenzied dance.

The craft descended with a growl, blades slicing the air with a mechanical rhythm that doesn't belong in paradise. Jason Wells, wearing mirrored aviators, stepped out, his boots crunching against the tarmac.

Inside the villa, the den is quiet but the mood is tense. A large QLED screen flickers with news from Washington about Hamilton's death, Mallory's swearing-in, and the world pivoting on a silent axis. The room is cool, comfortably modern, and still, as if holding its breath.

Jessica sits beside Taylor on the low leather couch, her eyes fixed on the screen. Her hand trembles slightly as she reaches for her tea. Maggie moves quietly between them, pouring from a delicate porcelain pot, her movements precise and practiced, as if ceremony could anchor them against the tide of change.

Lori sits nearby, cross-legged on the rug, a children's book open in her lap. She traces the illustrations with her finger, unaware or perhaps simply unwilling to understand the weight that hangs in the room. Maggie gave her the book earlier that morning, a gift wrapped in quiet kindness.

Wells enters the room without announcement, his presence cutting through the hush like a blade. Jessica turns to look at him and says softly, her voice catching, "We lost him, Jason."

He didn't answer at first, just moved with measured steps to stand across from her, his expression unreadable. "I know," he said at last. "It's complicated. Can we talk?"

Taylor, ever attuned to the unspoken, reached out and gently took the teacup from Jessica's hand. He placed it on the table and gave her a subtle nod toward the terrace.

Jessica rose without a word. The room seemed to hold its breath as she followed Wells through the open glass doors, stepping into the full blaze of the morning sun. The sea stretched before them, vast and indifferent, its surface glittering like a secret too large to hold.

From the doorway, Maggie watched. She knew something was wrong the moment Wells arrived. Her gaze followed Jessica's silhouette as it moved into the light, elegant, composed, but carrying something fragile beneath the surface. Without a word, Maggie walked to the couch, knelt beside Lori, and placed a gentle hand on the child's shoulder. She didn't know what Jessica was hearing from Wells, but she knew it was bad.

On the terrace, the wind moved through the bougainvillea, scattering petals. Wells spoke, his voice low, heavy, "This is a hard one, Jessica. Mark sold out to the wrong people and they took him down."

She turned her face slightly, the wind catching strands of her hair and lifting them like silk threads in the light. "Then he died chasing ghosts," she said, her voice sharp, the edge of grief cutting through. "He didn't even have all the data. Who pulled the trigger? Was it you?"

"No," Wells said. Then, after a pause, "But we cancelled out China."

Jessica closed her eyes. The sun was warm on her skin, but inside, a cold ache was blooming. "God, poor Lori," she whispered. "She's got no one."

Wells reached for her hand, and for a moment, his mask slipped. "She's got you."

The words struck her like a bell, clear, resonant, and impossible to ignore. Jessica turned, her eyes shining, not with tears but with something older. Resolve. Grace.

From the open doors, Wells watched her walk back inside. She moved to Lori without hesitation, knelt beside her, and gently took the book from her hands. Then, with a quiet strength, she lifted the child into her arms. Jessica whispered something only a mother would say, something soft and private and meant to last.

Lori rested her head against Jessica's shoulder, and in that moment, the bond was sealed. Not by blood, but by something stronger. Jessica turned and walked slowly from the room, carrying the child with her.

Taylor stood motionless, his eyes following them. Maggie remained kneeling, her hand still resting where Lori had been. Wells stepped into the room behind them, his presence now quieter, as if something had settled in him too. For a long moment, no one spoke.

The screen continued its quiet broadcast. The world was still turning. But in that villa on St. George, something had changed. Something had begun. The Game had changed.

The Oval Office

Once a chamber of reverence and legacy, the Oval Office now felt like a war room, its silence heavy with the weight of new power.

President Douglas Mallory stood beneath the gaze of history, the portraits of past leaders watching with painted eyes, their judgment mute. Around him, the quiet hum of advisors faded as he raised a hand, firm, final. "Clear the room," he said, his voice a low command. Only Colonel Martin Kane remained, standing sentinel near the fireplace.

Mallory's private iPhone buzzed, a vibration that seemed to echo off the walls like a warning. He answered, turning slightly away, as if the voice on the other end might burn through the air.

A growl, metallic and venomous, coiled through the line. "Your first full day on the job," it said, "and you conspire to fuck us."

It was the voice of the American Director Malcom Trent, faceless, but known. A whisper in the marrow of the nation's bones.

"That was my predecessor," Mallory replied, calm as a glacier. "But I approved of it. I have an obligation to the security of this nation, not to Chinese Asia or the consortium."

A pause. Then venom again. "You're forgetting who you are."

Mallory turned, his reflection caught in the darkened glass of the Resolute Desk. "I'm President of the all-powerful United States," he said. "And the game has changed."

A hiss, sharp and final. "This is not over. We're why you're sitting where you are. And you know it."

Mallory hung up.

Outside, dusk fell over the world like a blade, swift, cold, and absolute.

The Compound, St. George

Night cloaked the compound in velvet shadows. The stars above St. George blinked like distant sentinels, indifferent to the violence creeping below.

At the gate, two guards fell without a sound. Four figures, black-clad and faceless, slipped through the perimeter like phantoms. They moved like military ghosts, precise, their breath shallow, their mission sharp. At their head, Kamila Dimitriova, masked and merciless, led them forward. Her Glock 9 caught a glint of moonlight, a sliver of steel in the dark.

They fanned out toward the main villa, shadows moving among shadows.

Inside Jessica's tower bedroom, the air was still, too still. She stirred, a whisper of movement beneath the linen sheets. Her eyes opened. She listened. Then came the faintest creak.

Operative Panke Yassov crept forward, sack in hand, his breath shallow behind his mask. He hovered over the bed, a predator in the hush.

But before he could strike—motion. Blinding, brutal.

Jessica lashed out, a judo chop cracking through the night like thunder. Yassov hit the floor hard, dazed. He tried to rise, but was too slow.

Maggie was already on him. She moved like a cobra, silent, coiled, explosive. One fluid motion and he was airborne, then slammed against the wall. Unconscious.

Another attacker lunged. One swift strike to the throat and the attacker crumpled in silence.

Elsewhere in the villa, Dimitriova had found her way inside Atlantis, the control center. She moved with surgical purpose, scooping up drives, scanning data.

Then click. Cold steel pressed to her forehead.

"Everything back in its place…with care," Wells said with malice.

Behind him, another Russian operative lay unconscious, his body crumpled like a discarded coat. Two Secret Service agents emerged from the shadows, wordless and efficient, binding Dimitriova with practiced hands.

"Bring her up to the lounge," Wells said, already turning and climbing the stairs.

Back in Jessica's bedroom, silence returned, but not peace.

Maggie stood over Yassov's body. He stirred. Then, in a sudden burst, he leapt to his feet and dove through the open shuttered window, gone into the black of night.

Maggie darted forward, then stopped, frustrated. She stared into the dark, her breath sharp. Behind her Wells entered, brushing glass from his sleeve.

"Well done, you, even if you let him get away," he said with a chuckle, the sound dry as dust.

"We do what we can." She winked, a trace of fire in her voice.

"Which is quite a bit, Major Margaret Sexton-Smyth. Former British SAS. I ran a background check. Impressive."

"Well, you knew it wasn't the tea," she replied, not without pride.

Then a pause. A shift. They looked around. Jessica was gone.

They rushed to Lori's room. she slept soundly, untouched by chaos, her breath even, her dreams unbroken.

"I know where she may be," Wells said, already moving.

Maggie followed, their steps echoing through the villa's marble halls. They found her in the lounge, seated and composed, across from Kamila Dimitriova. The Russian leaned back, amused, her bindings no match for her poise. Two agents flanked her, silently observing, like statues.

Wells stepped forward, his voice smooth, "It seems your associates have left you to face the music."

Dimitriova smiled, switching to English. "I apologize for their awkward social skills. We were merely here to invite Dr. Peake to join us for a while as a guest of the new UFST."

Maggie folded her arms. "With no bloodshed. How very un-Russian."

Dimitriova's eyes gleamed. "We have a new kind of psychic surgery. One injection, and we get everything in your brain. No coercion."

Jessica stared her down, eyes like glass under flame. "You were trying to avail yourselves of my technology? Premier Karpov will soon know that I'm sending it to him intact, through you."

Jessica walked to Wells and indicating Dimitriova said, "Get her out of here, and make certain the agents take her to Washington."

She turned and walked away, with measured, unshaken steps.

Across the villa, she entered her office, sat before her desk, and tapped a hidden sequence of keys. A soft hum answered her touch. The holographic interface bloomed to life and Taylor's face appeared in the shimmer.

"Taylor," she said calmly. "Time to bring out the Cylinders."

Behind her, in the doorway, Wells froze. His voice was quiet. Disbelieving. "The Cylinders?"

THIRTY-FOUR

The Irenic cylinders

JESSICA STOOD IN HER CONTROL CENTER, her gleaming sanctuary of code and conscience. Expecting Taylor to arrive any moment, she cleared an area on a table placed close to the large window displaying the ocean's splendor.

Taylor arrives carrying a sleek black case, and Jessica gestures to the table. Taylor puts it down and opens it with quiet ceremony. Nestled within are ten titanium cylinders, each sealed in its own segment, like relics of a forgotten future. He unsheathes one and hands it to her.

She holds it delicately, reverently. The cylinder, five inches wide and fourteen inches tall, gleams. A monolith in miniature, humming with invisible power.

"Irenic Cylinders," she says, her voice steady, her eyes distant. "Every major power wants my Neutrino Formulations." Holding it toward the ocean light that shimmers across the titanium surface, she continues, "They're willing to kidnap, maim, even kill to get them. So, we make it easy."

She glances at Maggie who stands behind Wells, silent and in awe of Jessica. "Maggie, It's time. Discreetly get these little time bombs moving."

She hands a cylinder to Taylor. "These aren't gifts of peace, John. They're triggers, meant to reveal each nation's nature. Some cautious. Some calculating. Some, like Pakistan already poised to act."

Taylor takes the cylinder, focused on what Jessica is about to say.

"The Vernal Equinox is our global meeting point. A poetic, powerful choice, it symbolizes balance and rebirth. It's the perfect moment to reset the rules of global power." She smiles, sighs.

"Let's get it moving. The world's already watching."

Taylor places the cylinder back in the case with the others and snaps it shut, then hands it to Maggie.

"Maggie, one cylinder goes to each consulate. They'll know how to get them to their heads of state, wherever they are." Jessica looks at them both, wondering if they truly understand.

"The cylinders are themselves like modern-day sacred relics, imbued with mystery, power, and the threat of misuse is evident. Their design and function will evoke both reverence and fear. They're my holy Grail."

"And Maggie," Jessica says emphatically, "make sure the printed notes are included in each package. You know where they are."

"They'll force every nuclear power to confront its own paranoia," Taylor added. "as well as its pride and its potential."

Jessica knows she is now a compelling protagonist, a visionary, wielding not just technology, but diplomacy, and a kind of mythic resolve. The Cylinders are her brilliant narrative device, equal parts Pandora's box and olive branch. She feels like a modern-day Prometheus, offering fire, but with a warning. Her voice is authoritative, symbolic, and emotionally restrained and she knows it.

Four days later

A fire is burning in Premier Alexi Karpov's private area at the Kremlin. An elderly woman throws another log into the fire positions it with a large antique metal poker before leaving the room.

Alexi is holding the titanium cylinder he's been sent, turning it over and over. Across from him, Ivgeny Maxim and Kamila Dimitriova sit like chess masters considering an impossible gambit.

The Premier looks over to Dimitriova and says, "I am glad they let you go. I had to let quite a few rogues go to get you back."

"It's well appreciated, sir. We were told the algorithms are inside each cylinder," Dimitriova explains holding up the note that came with the package. "There are also instructions for how to apply them."

She hands the note to the Premier, adding, "All nine nuclear nations have received similar packages. The single stipulation attached to this 'gift' is that no one opens the cylinders until the NPT meeting on the Vernal Equinox."

"And we're expected to play by the rules when no one else intends to play by the rules?" Karpov scoffs.

No. 10 Downing Street

Prime Minister Ian Gifford circles his desk, eyeing the cylinder like it might explode. His MI6 liaison stands nearby, silent.

"So," Gifford mutters, "we're handed the most critical peacetime technology in the world by this science Svengali like it's some Christmas popper? And she's a Yank at that! Then we're told every other nuclear nation has one just like it? Doug Mallory must be crapping razor blades.

"The chosen date for the NPT meeting must be rich with symbolism," he continues. "I'll just bet the Vernal Equinox represents balance, equality, and transition, since Dr. Peake's entire plan hinges on these themes."

The Oval Office

President Douglas Mallory clutches the cylinder he received in one hand like it's a grenade. His other hand holds the crumpled note. His face is flushed, his temper boiling. Nicholas Porter and

Georgina Milomett, Mallory's assistant, flank him, trying to calm the storm.

Mallory's on the verge of a complete meltdown, Georgina thinks as her boss finally speaks.

"That double-dealing bitch!" Mallory snarls. "If she had balls, I'd castrate her!"

"Give us time," Porter pleads. "We can crack the code well ahead of Geneva."

"Crack it? Hell, *I'll* crack it!" Mallory hurls the cylinder and it ricochets off the wall with a metallic scream as his staffers dive for cover.

Jerusalem

Prime Minister Josef Meyerson watches as his scientific team scans the cylinder with thermographic precision, but cannot penetrate it.

"Our thermography is unable to see anything," a scientist reports, "But if we break the seal, the cylinder will flood with ink and drench the scroll within according to the accompanying note."

Meyerson smiles, impressed. "Ingenious. Leave it intact."

Beijing

Premier Yang Bin Rong contemplates the cylinder like a philosopher with a puzzle box. Hui Chen stands beside him, analytical and calm. "It appears Dr. Peake has her own version of a Chinese box," Hui says.

"With respect," Yang replies, "enlighten me as to how this came about. We've used every means available to try to eliminate Jessica Peake and pirate her technology. Now she just hands it over as part of a Universal Peace Plan with equal access for all nuclear nations?"

"I suspect she wants to create a level playing field," Hui offers.

"But level for whom?" Yang muses. "She's playing the nations against each other, using our fear of exclusion to make us reveal ourselves. The harder we try, the weaker we look—and she damn well knows it. Clever girl."

He adjusts his collar and continues, "Dr. Jessica Peake walks the line between oracle and engineer. Her calm, measured demeanor contrasts beautifully with the chaos she may ultimately unleash, not through violence, but through possibility."

Paris

President Nicolas Dimentiere stands on the steps of the Élysée Palace, and tightens the belt of his overcoat as he readies himself to address a skeptical press as a cold northly wind cuts across the courtyard.

"From what I can see," he declares, "these 'Irenic Peace Cylinders' sent by the American scientist Dr. Jessica Peake are as phony as she is. A woman who cannot even control her own technology now wants to dictate our nuclear policy, without proof, without demonstration to do what she claims she can do."

Cameras flash, and reporters' questions are shouted. "I'm sorry, ladies and gentlemen, there are just too many unanswered questions at the moment and I can tell you nothing further," he turns and steps back into the palace.

Atlantis compound

Jessica has been watching global reactions to what she's done. Each leader's response reveals their nation's stance: Karpov's cynicism, Gifford's sarcasm, Mallory's rage, and Dimentiere's dismissal all contrast Meyerson's measured admiration and Yang's strategic respect. *I haven't just distributed technology,* Jessica muses, *I gave them all mirrors.*

The night hums with potential as Jessica sits before her console. Taylor and Maggie stand nearby, all three having witnessed the Paris press conference. Maggie and Taylor, though silent, are witnesses to Jessica's resolve.

"It's a valid criticism," Jessica admits. "Can I walk my walk and talk my talk? Hmm… It's time to find out if my cellular transformation carries a consciousness with it."

She turns to her keyboard, its new bank of keys gleaming pallid ivory, and begins to type. Each deft keystroke is a note in a musical score only she can hear. Though it's not music, not exactly. Something close though—a symphony of code, a concerto of intent.

As she works, there is a shift in the room's energy. An unseen current stirs a silent symphony of energy, vibrating at the edge of perception. Neutrinos pour forth in an invisible deluge, saturating the room, dissolving the boundaries of space and self. In the span of a nanosecond, the radiant tide ascends, a dawn not of light but of pure force, sweeping outward to envelop the lab, the house, and the entire compound.

Taylor and Maggie stand suspended in awe, rendered wordless by the revelation, and the staggering, transcendent power that emerges when Jessica and the neutrinos become one.

Then, across the island of St. George, people step out of shops and restaurants, pausing mid-step, mid-sentence, mid-thought to look up, awestruck, as light, sound, and motion converge in a miracle of transformation. The beaches seem to darken under a sullen sky, even as a rainbow arcs across the horizon. Dr. Jessica Peake has begun to walk her walk and talk her talk.

THIRTY-FIVE

Lake Band-e Amir

A CHAIN OF SIX DEEP BLUE LAKES, a natural wonder nestled in the heart of central Afghanistan, had long been celebrated for their serene beauty. Declared the country's first national park, the area stood in stark contrast to the trauma of eons of war. Now, the park served as the improbable setting for something even more profound: the metaphysical reconstitution of the village of Ab Barik.

There it was, unmistakable, on the edge of the lake, visible now to Phillip as he observed from his satellite station. He blinked. He had never seen this before. Could it be another miraculous restoration, just as what had been reported with Dr. Peake?

Phillip hesitated, then he zoomed in for a closer look. What he saw caused him to pick up his cellphone and dial.

After a series of countless transfers, Jessica, seated at her desk, was finally on the line with Phillip. As she listened, she turned on her horoscopic screen and there it was. Stunned, she stared. *Transported once, survived, and now?*

"How can such a power transform everything cell by cell, matter by matter? Her words are spoken softly, more to the screen than to Phillip. "It's like primal creation—creating, but not destroying its creations."

Within less than an hour, Jessica had organized a film crew to be dispatched to the location.

The wind rushed through the open door of a hovering helicopter, its blades slicing the alpine air above Lake Band-e Amir. A man leaned behind a mounted camera, his lens trained on the vast expanse below. The lake glimmered like a mirror beneath the fading amber of evening light, framed by the stark majesty of the Afghan mountains.

From this height, the camera captured what no eye had seen before: a transformation not of time, but of space and memory.

The helicopter swept low, skimming inches above the lake's surface. A fine particle storm, like stardust caught in a divine breath, erupted along the shoreline. It shimmered, then thickened, coalescing into form. Structures rose from the sand and gravel beaches, as if time were rewinding.

The village of Ab Barik had reassembled itself with impossible precision. Disintegrating huts reformed. A tank found its original position, half-buried in gravel. A NATO Jeep beside it. The villagers, men, women and children stood once more alongside NATO Rangers and two IS combatants, all as if reborn.

It was as though the earth itself, hesitant to recall what was lost, had finally exhaled, restoring what had been erased. The routines of daily living resumed, as though the long absence was merely a pause in the ongoing story.

It was, in its way, reminiscent of how Jessica Peake had appeared in India—unexpected, almost spectral, yet entirely real. The people of Ab Barik, like Jessica, seemed to have crossed an invisible threshold, returning changed but determined to claim their place in the world once more.

Two young girls, stand barefoot at the lake's edge as the last of the white light dissipates. Their wide eyes catch the sun's final rays as waves lap gently at their feet. Behind them, three NATO Rangers lean beside the tank's tracks. One of them, hardened by war, looks utterly lost.

A young boy, the one who haunted Jessica Peake's memory like a ghost of guilt, was whole again. Not a scar marked his skin. He ran into the arms of his mother, who stood alive, healed, and radiant. They embraced, spinning in a circle of joy.

Nearby, an IS fighter trembled, his weapon forgotten in the sand. He turned to face Mecca, knelt and prayed, not in surrender, but in reverence.

A helicopter touched down on a flat stretch of beach, and a news crew disembarked, cameras already rolling. Microphones rose like flowers toward the light as the reporters began to document what would soon be called the greatest unexplained restoration in modern history.

Geneva, Switzerland, three days later

Flags from 193 nations snapped in a brisk alpine wind, flanking the sleek architecture of the United Nations headquarters. Fountains roared as throngs of protesters chanted in a dozen languages. Cameras flashed and the press corps surged outside the gates with a tide of questions waiting for answers.

A BBC newscaster stood before the chaos, framed by marble and sky, saying, "Could it be that Wonder Woman is no longer a fable of American comics? Has she become an unsettling reality that the USA has let loose upon the world? Or, has she, as she claims, brought us the last best instrument of peace?"

Across the plaza, an ABC anchor delivered a live broadcast with little interruption from the protestors. "The mystery of Ab Barik has been solved in ways that no one quite expected. And the architect of the most controversial scientific technology in a thousand years has finally come forward. The question that remains: is this a force for good or the source of Armageddon? Has Dr. Jessica Peake become the most powerful woman in the world?"

A sleek black limousine pulled to the curb. The rear door was opened by a security guard. Two others stood on either side of the vehicle.

Dr. Peake stepped out, composed and luminous. A figure of paradox: scientist and symbol, rebel and redeemer. She acknowledged her security as cameras swarmed her like bees to nectar.

"The world press lies to you. I am definitely not responsible for finding a way to restore the village at Ab Barik," she said, her voice calm. "Yes, I was responsible for the entire village vanishing: soldiers, tanks, weapons, and villagers. I was only trying to break down the physical structures at the molecular level to see if I could eliminate the destructive arms of our world."

She paused, then looked directly into the ABC camera and continued, "That's why I'm here today. I have no more to say at this time."

Accompanied by her security, she walked up the steps of the United Nations. A voice behind her cried out, "Dr. Peake, will you make time to visit the village?"

Jessica hesitated...then decided to ignore the question and then entered the building. Security opened a large door for her, and she stepped into a private conference chamber. Mallory was already there, flanked by his advisors. His expression was carved from stone.

"I could have you arrested right now for betrayal of national security," he said. "And I should."

Jessica didn't flinch. "Oh, good evening, Mr. President. I suppose you *could* do that," she replied mockingly, "but you can't afford the optics. It wouldn't look right to arrest someone for trying to broker nuclear peace."

"God damn it!" Mallory said, slamming his fist on the table, "This is *not* what we agreed on! Thanks to you, we've lost all strategic advantage. You're a traitor to your country."

He approached her, getting in her face. "Peake, you're a scientist whose invention blurs the line between science and miracle, but let's not forget whose nasty, sticky thumb we are both under."

She met his fury with something colder—clarity. "Look at it this way, Mr. President. I'm your creature, win or lose. Just hope to God I don't embarrass you in public."

The comment was met by silence. Outside, the world watched.

THIRTY-SIX

The Irenic Principle

THE CHAMBER EXUDES QUIET AUTHORITY, its soaring ceilings amplifying every subtle movement. A hush blankets the space, broken only by the soft rustle of papers and the low murmur of anticipation. Arrayed in sweeping tiers, the world's most powerful leaders—the G-22—occupy their seats with a gravity befitting the moment. Faces are drawn, postures rigid; skepticism and caution flicker in every glance exchanged, as if the very air is charged with consequence.

In the front rows, the representatives of the nuclear nations are especially still. Arms metaphorically crossed, they carry the invisible weight of their arsenals like a second skin. They are the primary audience for Jessica Peake's ultimatum. The unspoken gravity of her presence is felt most acutely here, among those who hold the fate of the world in their hands.

Jessica steps to the dais. Her demeanor is calm, composed. She is dressed simply, but her presence radiates the weight of a thousand pages of research and a thousand sleepless nights.

Behind her, a holographic display shimmers to life—showing a slow, elegant rotation of the Irenic Peace Cylinder, suspended in mid-air like a sacred artifact.

"Thank you," she begins, her voice clear and resolute. "Thank you for coming. And thank you to those of you who have managed it, for suspending disbelief."

She pauses. The silence that follows is intentional, commanding. "You represent the twenty-two most economically influential nations on Earth. Nine of you possess one hundred percent of the world's nuclear capability, and now you hold in your hands an Irenic Peace Cylinder, calibrated and ready."

"This represents a technological leap," she continues as she gestures to the floating projection of the cylinder, "a leap capable of neutralizing nuclear threats without violence."

A murmur ripples through the room. Some delegates lean forward, while others sit back.

Jessica continues, her voice unwavering. "Ten days from now, on the Vernal Equinox, I will finalize the code that activates each cylinder. Once it's completed, I will transmit the final key. That key will initiate a particle shield that will provide a new kind of defense system—one that intercepts and neutralizes nuclear attacks from any source. There will be no retaliation, no escalation. Just silence."

She raises her right arm and traces a slow, deliberate arc one hundred and eighty degrees across the assembly. "This is a one-time offer," she says, drawing a metaphorical line in the sand. Holding up a gleaming cylinder for all to see, she continues, "This madness, this spiral toward destruction, must end. And we can end it. But only if we act together in concert."

This speech, transmitted across the globe impacts all who hear it. In a New York nightclub, dancers freeze mid-motion to listen. In a London pub, the barman raises the television volume. On a factory floor in Mumbai, machines hum as workers stare in silence. In a Tahitian breakfast bar, forks rest motionless on porcelain plates.

The world listens and Jessica's voice echoes across continents. "I know some of you have already tried to crack the codes. And failed. Let this be your warning. Respect this opportunity, and mark the date March 20 on your schedules, because on that date you will all be able to open your cylinders."

The Pakistani Premier pushes himself out of his seat, shaking and angry. He points to her and the cylinder and shouts, "Peake, what's your ultimate plan and when do we get to see what's hidden in ours?" He does not sit down.

"As I just mentioned to you all, you will be able to open them on March 20th, not a moment sooner." Her gaze steady, she concludes, "The world will be watching." Then, without haste, she turns and walks away.

Behind her, the chamber erupts. Not in applause, but in chaos. Delegates turn to their interpreters. Words fly like shrapnel.

"Arrogant bitch!" hisses French delegate Nicolas Dementiere. "Who does she think she is, issuing ultimatums to us?"

"She's a woman," snaps Kim Pun Tang of Korea. "Alone. On an island. She's overplayed her hand. She's a target now."

Mallory stands, calm and deliberate. "Her compound is located in a national park on the island of St. George, in the U.S. Virgin Islands. Any military action against it will be considered an attack on U.S. territory."

Ian Gifford of Great Britain leans forward, fingers steepled. "Shouldn't we at least hear her out? What if she's right?"

"I'm willing," says Yang of China.

"I am not!" thunders President Singh of Pakistan. "Pakistan will not have its nuclear sovereignty held hostage by a woman." He storms out followed by his delegation.

France and Saudi Arabia soon join him in protest, marching out beneath the glare of international cameras.

Outside, the media frenzy ignites.

CNN calls it a "stunning pronouncement" that demands "a tremendous leap of faith from nations with fractured trust." FOX News labels it "the political equivalent of poking a hornet's nest."

MSNBC airs footage allegedly leaked by Russian hackers—grainy, terrifying images of a whaler factory ship and the floating Island of plastic disintegrating in a cascade of light, undone by the same neutrino technology Jessica now offers the world.

And from the White House lawn, a spokesperson confirms what many had suspected: the U.S. has been working with Jessica Peake in secret. The country's leaders not only drawn to the promise of peace, but to the potential to erase billions of tons of waste from the planet in a single stroke.

Jessica Peake has spoken. Now, the world must decide whether to listen.

THIRTY-SEVEN

The threshold

EVENING FELL OVER THE ISLAND. Inside Atlantis, the hidden control center where glass and steel met the sea in quiet defiance of the world's chaos, Jessica stands before a panoramic screen as the final flickers of the White House broadcast dissolve into static.

Behind her, Jason Wells shifts his weight, arms folded, eyes never leaving her. "An olive branch from our beloved Potus?" he said, voice edged with irony. "So, take him up on it."

Jessica doesn't turn, but says, "We talked. I'll admit. He was less of an asshole than usual."

Jason raises an eyebrow. "Considering you just issued an ulti-matum to every nuclear power on Earth, I'd say he's being gen-erous. Half of them want you dead. And it's my job to keep you breathing."

She smiled faintly. "I never said it would be easy."

"It's not the nations I worry about," he said, more quietly now. "It's the Consortium. They don't forgive. And they certainly don't forget."

"I know," she whispered. "I'm sorry, Jason…"

But he was already gone.

In his place, a softer presence entered. Lori climbed into Jessica's lap as if drawn there, her small arms wrapping around Jessica's waist with the trust only a child can offer.

"Hi, Jessica. Are you going to play your 'save the world' game again?"

Jessica kissed the crown of her head. "Yes, sweetheart. That's exactly what I'm going to do." She hugged her tight, then gently put her down. "Run upstairs. Maggie will have your favorite lemonade waiting for you."

Later that evening Jessica's Range Rover moved through the gates of her villa compound, speeding toward the Neutrino Hangar. Waiting by the open gate was Taylor, his silhouette sharp against the floodlights.

"There are a trillion creatures in there waiting for a mindmeld," he said, pocketing the micro disk she handed him. "Can you do it this time?"

"You mean, if I love them, will they love me back?"

He nodded. "Something like that."

"I'm all in."

High above, hidden on the mountainside, a swarthy, bearded sniper watched her through the crosshairs of a Dragunov SVD rifle fixed to a bipod. His finger hovered. He didn't fire. Not yet. But he was locked in.

Too late. Jessica and Taylor had already vanished into the vast interior of the Hanger. They moved quickly, reached the exterior of the Collecting Chamber and stopped. No words were needed. She hugged Taylor with final resolve, entered her codes and entered.

She stood in silent reverence, confronted with the vast metal Globe she now called Mother. She moved with practiced precision, her fingers dancing across the console. The codes responded like old friends. There within the Globe she witnessed trillions of radiant vibrating particles of light that left the Globe and passed through her body until she was no longer flesh and bone. She had become light—she was one with its radiance.

She watched herself disintegrate, cell by cell, then dissolve into a cascade of brilliance. There was no pain, only a profound release, as if every boundary she'd ever known simply melted away. Awareness expanded, stretching beyond the limits of flesh, until she was everywhere at once: a consciousness woven into the very fabric of the globe.

The chamber faded, replaced by a sensation of infinite space. Jessica's thoughts flickered like the radiant particles, each memory and feeling refracted through new dimensions. She sensed the pulse of the Globe: steady, ancient, maternal, welcoming her into its embrace. She was both herself and something more, a luminous thread in a vast and intricate tapestry.

For a moment, she saw the world as the Globe did: networks of energy, rivers of possibility flowing through darkness. In a flash of insight, she understood the purpose of her journey and the legacy she was about to inherit. And as she hovered on the edge of becoming, the last fragments of her old self shimmered into nothingness, and Jessica surrendered to the light. She was reborn.

She eventually left Atlantis and returned to her vehicle. The sniper was gone.

THIRTY-EIGHT

Somewhere unseen

Washington, DC

PRESIDENT MALLORY STARED at a wall of screens in the Situation Room. Beside him, Secretary Hamm leaned in, whispering urgently.

Mallory picked up the secure line and Jessica answered.

"Well, hotshot," he said. "India's going hot. They'll strike Pakistan within 48 hours. Pakistan will pre-empt. Which means—"

"I get it," Jessica interrupted calmly. "The U.S. will have to retaliate in defense of India. Such chaos! And mother Earth, no one has even mentioned her."

"This is on you now, Little Miss Save-the-Planet. I don't know if your Neutrino magic trick has a chance in hell. But if you can work it, we need it." He paused, then shouted: "And we needed it yesterday!"

"I understand."

"I think, at last, you do." He hung up and immediately dialed again. "Get me Premier Yang."

The Villa

That evening, Jessica stood on the open balcony of her villa, facing the mountains. The sky was painted in amber and ash. She paced, her hand trailing along the railing, her mind a storm of consequences and impossible choices.

Somewhere unseen, the sniper adjusted his scope.

Maggie appeared, pulling Jessica gently toward the door. "For once," she said softly, "listen to Jason Wells. You have promises to keep. And miles to go before you sleep."

They turned to go inside when they heard a crack split the air.

The sniper had begun to squeeze the trigger, when his head snapped back. A single shot echoed across the island. On a distant ridge, Jason Wells exhaled behind the scope of his Barrett M82. The weight of the moment collapsed into his shoulders.

March 20ᵗʰ

In Rawalpindi, Prime Minister Singh stands before a digital war map glowing with red and amber lines. His generals await his command, after having opened the cylinder. "The cylinder is a bluff she is holding the world for ransom," he says flatly. "There's nothing inside. No algorithm. No miracle. Just pressure."

A general hesitates then nods. "Then we proceed?"

He stares with a flicker of doubt at the blinking outline of Delhi. "The world waits for Peake's promised peace. We will move before they realize it's a myth."

"Korea is focused on Taiwan," another aide adds, look pointing to the map. "The Americans will be watching the Pacific, not us."

The Premiers eyes narrow. "Then we strike. Before the world remembers how dangerous we truly are."

Consortium Headquarters, New York

Sir Peter Murton and Malcolm Trent sit in silence, their eyes fixed on the open cylinder teetering at the edge of the oval oak table. With a swift motion, Murton leans forward and catches the cylinder just before it falls. He rises, walks calmly to the open window, and without a word, hurls the device outside toward an old stone well. It arcs cleanly through the air, dropping into the darkness below.

Without looking back to Trent, he says, "Mallory is going to pay for this."

Sir Murton opens his silver cigarette case and lights up.

Beijing

The sky is a cold slate gray, and the city hums beneath Premier Yang's feet as he stands in his tower, hands clasped behind his back, eyes fixed on a holographic globe.

Hui Chen enters, urgency in her voice. "Pakistan, Israel, Russia and North Korea are all preparing to launch."

Yang nodded. "Let them. China will not. Sun Tzu said, 'If facing enemies on two fronts, encourage them to fight each other. Defeat the survivor. Then claim the peace.'"

He turned to her. "We will broadcast Jessica Peake's Irenic Promise on all media. If she delivers, we win. If she fails, we win. In all cases—we win." With a wave of his hand, the globe vanished.

Later that evening

The BBC cut into global programming, and world's televisions, radios, laptops carried the same content: Jessica Peake.

"To all nations," she began, "two days ago, I announced that on the Vernal Equinox, I would deliver the final algorithms for the Irenic Shield coded to protect all nations from nuclear attack from any source."

Across the globe, people watched: students in Yale lounges, farmers in Irish kitchens, soldiers in Iraqi outposts, families in Mexican cantinas. A bar in San Francisco. A Mosque in London. An Aboriginal family in the Australian outback. Even Messiah elders huddled around an old, weathered transistor.

"I know there are those who fear this shield. They feel threatened by peace. But I've discovered something: the Irenic Principle responds to our collective consciousness."

Her voice rang out on jumbotrons in Shanghai, in UN chambers in Brussels, in clubs in Lagos. "The power of Neutrino particle penetration is an extension of the human desire for peace, harmony and love. That essence is you. It is infinite. A reservoir I can tap into, if we apply it together."

In Real Madrid stadium, the crowd locked hands. In Phoenix, a black church choir sang with abandon. In the Outback, Elders watched silently, firelight flickering on their faces.

"From now until midnight GMT," Jessica said, "focus if you are able on that feeling of love. Reach out to one another. Embrace the light within every breath."

She stood before her console, the screens around her pulsing with energy, then turned and looked at a framed print of a detail of the Cantina drawn and signed by her great grandfather.

Turning back she spoke directly to the screen and with a knowing smile, "You are the Force. Within every breath. Let go and focus."

She closed her eyes, hands poised. "One last thought. Trust me. If you focus on that feeling of love, you will give the Irenic Shield the spin it needs to fulfill its purpose: to protect our Mother Earth."

No. 10 Downing Street

Prime Minister Ian Gifford leaned back, half-smiling. "Well, that was some Tinkerbell speech," he muttered. "Millions locking arms and singing Kumbaya? At least she's bought us some time. Who wants to be the first trigger-happy bastard after that speech?"

Atlantis

Jessica is now the conductor of creation's concerto, standing before her console. Taylor appeared on the screen and asked, "How about it, boss? Ready to dance?"

She smiled. "It's now or never. Let's tango."

She initiated a sequence of commands on the console, her hands moving with practiced efficiency. The command center responded instantly. Holographic displays materialized in synchronized layers, illuminating the room with streams of real-time data. Each screen offered a unique perspective of energy flux readings, quantum resonance patterns, and live visualizations of the Collection Chamber.

Inside the chamber, the particle infusion system activated, meticulously orchestrating the controlled Neutrino storm. Parameters were maintained with exacting precision, temperature, magnetic containment, and flow rate all monitored and adjusted by her expert oversight. The replication process unfolded seamlessly, a testament to the advanced technology and her unparalleled expertise.

She directed the storm with unwavering focus, channeling it not just through technology, but through intention. Through light, through will, and through an unflinching love for the world she was sworn to protect. She knew exactly what she was doing. And yet, even she was momentarily awed by the magnitude of what was taking shape.

On the monitors, waves of radiant, multicolored light surged upward, rising through the atmosphere in silent, accelerating pulses. They climbed until they reached the edge of the stratosphere, then spread outward like the petals of a cosmic bloom.

Wells had been gazing at the horizon from Jessica's garden terrace, when the light caught his eye. He called out, urgency and wonder in his voice. "Maggie! Lori! Come see this!"

From the direction of the Neutrino Compound, a brilliant white light was rising, pure, steady, and impossibly vast.

Lori, barely able to contain herself, bounced on her toes and pointed. "Maggie, it looks like a giant white ice cream cone!"

Maggie said nothing, her breath caught in her chest. She was transfixed.

The light expanded, rippling outward until it covered the entire Northern Hemisphere. And then, in a moment that seemed to stretch beyond time, it wrapped itself around the planet. A shimmering, translucent shield now encased the Earth, suspended in grace and silence.

St. George Island pulsed at the heart of it all, a beacon of radiant energy. And for one breathless moment, Earth became a majestic sphere of light, silent, protected, and whole.

THIRTY-NINE

Irenic shield

IN A LARGE, ORNATE RESIDENCE in Pyongyang, Supreme Leader Kim Pun Tang sips his green tea with deliberate calm as a General stands stiffly nearby, delivering the latest intelligence. "A global meditation," the general reports. "A wave of unity and peace."

Kim sneers, setting his cup down with a soft clink. "Ah, brotherly love. How touching." He leans forward, voice sharpening. "How insulting." He wipes his mouth with a linen napkin, then tosses it aside.

"Time to break it up with a demonstration," he says coldly. "Hit Taiwan. They're a political orphan. There will be outrage, but no recourse. And China will be pleased."

Without another word, he returns to his breakfast. The General and the other two introverted soldiers scramble to obey.

In a vast missile silo somewhere in North Korea, the signal is given. A nuclear missile begins its launch sequence and engines roar to life.

Ankara

Inside the Presidential Complex, the President receives the message. He stands among his Generals, grim-faced. "North Korea is set to launch," he says. "That's our signal." He raises a clenched fist. "Death to Israel! I've waited for this for a long time."

A Turkish Revolutionary General echoes him. "Death to Israel!"

Jerusalem

Israeli Prime Minister Josef Meyerson listens as Intelligence Chief Hiram Itkin delivers the report. "Turkey's silos are two thousand six hundred kilometers away. If they launch, we won't stop them all."

Meyerson nods, resolute. "Pre-empt in forty-five minutes."

Nevada

The air in the desert silo compound is thick and metallic. Josh Green's fingers, calloused and trembling, dance nervously, fingering the key that hangs from his neck: a talisman, a curse, a promise for a number of Nuclear and Missle Operations.

Suddenly, the control panels erupt in a riot of color, lights blazing across the consoles like the Fourth of July. The chamber pulses with electricity, and alarms prick at Josh's nerves. Johnston, a younger sergeant, is hunched over the instruments, eyes darting, hands flying nervously.

"Sir," Johnston called, voice taut as piano wire, "I show a launch out of Pakistan."

Josh's heart hammered. "God damn it! Destination?"

Johnston's fingers fly, decoding the data, running numbers that might as well have been spells. In a whisper, barely audible above the cacophony, he says, "Looks like they've targeted India. And maybe…Washington."

Josh spat on the concrete floor, paranoia blooming. "Insanity! I knew we couldn't trust those kooks in their togas."

He yanked the key from his neck, the chain snapping against his collarbone. With a jerk, he opened the launch panel, slotting the key with trembling hands. Johnston stared, sweat beading on his forehead, disbelief etched deep in the lines around his eyes.

Josh turned, wild-eyed, lips curled in a snarl. "Insert your key, son!"

Johnston shook his head, voice cracking. "We can't. We haven't received orders." Now in panic. "The phone hasn't—"

"Fuck the phone!" Josh screams in anger and panic.

In a heartbeat, Josh's service revolver is out, the barrel dark and absolute. He levels it at Johnston, eyes burning. "Chain of command's right here! So, pull your god-damn key, or I'll blow your head off."

The tense moment stretched, the sirens screaming. Johnston's hands shook as he fumbled for his key, pulling it from its case, and slotting it home. Their eyes met: fear, anger, desperation, all reflected in the polished steel.

Josh's voice was a rasp, a curse and a command. "Ready… and… turn!"

Together, they twisted the keys a quarter-turn clockwise. The mechanism engaged with a sound like fate itself—a click, a shudder, the world tipping on its axis. Instantly, warning sirens and bells erupted, howling through the chamber, drowning out thought and hope.

But then—a new alarm blared, shriller than the rest. Across the main console, angry red letters flashed:

AUTHORIZATION FAILURE — LAUNCH INHIBITED

The system refused to yield. The missile remained locked down, held in check by the final safeguard: the missing presidential codes.

Josh stood, chest heaving, finger still on the trigger, as the machinery of annihilation trembled but did not awaken. Above, the world spun on, oblivious. Below, in the steel womb of the silo, duty and madness danced on the edge.

"Let's see if she can stop this one!" Josh screamed into John-ston's face, but the only answer was the unyielding wail of the alarms and the cold, silent refusal of the machine.

Washington, DC

Deep beneath the White House, in the PEOC bunker, President Douglas Mallory stood among his war-room staff. He just ended a call, and the room is tense, silent.

"Israel is launching to head off Turkey's strike," he says. "North Korea lets fly in thirty minutes. And Alexi Karpov is hitting Ukraine and Israel before noon our time."

He exhales sharply. "Fuck!"

Lieutenant Colonel Kane steps forward, carrying the nuclear codes "Football." Mallory raises a hand, stopping him.

"Not yet," he says, voice is heavy with conflict. "We can count-er-punch. Let's give peace and our friend Dr. Peake a chance."

Around him, advisors Hamm, Porter, and others stare in stunned silence.

"Believe me," Mallory adds, "no one is more surprised than me."

Stunned, Kane just holds his phone. "Sir, our silos in Nevada have been initiated. Without orders from you."

"That's not possible!" Mallory shouts. "How? That's treason!"

Porter, whose hands tremble with shock, replies, " It won't ignite, sir, not without your codes."

Atlantis

Wells stands observing Jessica's complete focus on the six screens that now show all ten silos from around the planet.

"How is that possible, Jessica?" Wells asks her, not understand-ing how she could possibly know where all the nuclear silos are located.

Jessica, losing no focus says, "Technology. You agents just don't keep up with the daily changes."

She observes the Korean silo open and at the same instant she is shocked to see the Nevada Silo open and let loose. She points it out to Wells and Maggie. "Here it comes—the nuclear tsunami! Washington's fired."

A missile bursts from a North Korean silo, streaking across the China Sea toward Taipei.

Israeli silos open. Missiles launch in response, including one from a submarine in the Mediterranean, all targeting Akbar.

From Pakistan, a missile launches toward Delhi, soaring over the jagged Karakoram Range.

In Russia, silos across Siberia and the Arctic erupt, sending missiles toward Ukraine, Israel, and even the West Coast of the United States.

Jessica stands with the fingers on both hands stretched wide across the console keys. She raises her head and speaks into a suspended mic as John looks on. "Now we need you. That love that you are within every breath is such a power. Combined with the Irenic Shield, it will save us. That is your true power."

The North Korean missile approaches Taipei, but never arrives. Instead, it slams into a shimmering Neutrino Shield and disintegrates instantly, particles dissolving into the vacuum.

Pakistan's missiles follow, each one sucked into a vortex of light and transformed into a harmless mist.

Israel's missiles meet a blinding wall of energy. They vanish on contact, with not even a trace left behind.

In the Neutrino Hangar, Taylor viewing various screens, is ecstatic. He is a dance of light, turning, observing his body becoming a trillion cells of white light. Disappearing and reappearing as he spins, enraptured.

Six Russian missiles scream through the upper atmosphere then collide with the Neutrino canopy and evaporate in a brilliant flash.

Around the world, the realization dawns: The Irenic Shield works. It is perfect. It is real.

On university campuses and in packed stadiums, people erupt in joy. The sky has become a canvas of light, a miracle witnessed by billions.

In an Irish farmhouse garden, two children dance as their parents play fiddle and spoons, laughter echoing through the air.

In Australia's red desert, bathed in moonlight, Aboriginal elders watch the fading energy with awe, then begin to dance to the low hum of a didgeridoo.

On the Ghats of Varanasi, thousands gather at the Ganges. Men, women, and children look skyward. The light is not destruction: it is a beacon.

In the PEOC bunker, the hardened defense staff breaks into cheers. The shield has held. The planet is safe.

President Mallory walks quietly to a corner and lowers his head into his hands, overcome. An aid walks towards him and hands him a phone. "I can't take this now," Mallory says, backing further into the corner of the bunker.

"They are insisting, Mr. President, sir."

"They?" He takes the phone and waves his hand, dismissing the aid.

He listens, then silently lets the phone drop. It was the commission, still demanding from him. He had given them Jessica, but she gave them nothing. In the silence she left behind, Mallory understood too late the cost of his choice. The truth bloomed like ash in his chest, bitter and inescapable.

The next morning, Maggie savored a much-needed cup of strong Irish breakfast tea while her favorite BBC news played quietly in the background. Channel Four's reports were always concise. Just the way she liked them.

She leaned in as the announcer's calm voice relayed the astonishing update: "Many nations have expressed utter disbelief. Not only have all launched nuclear warheads been destroyed, but reports are coming in that rockets stored in underground caves and reinforced chambers have also been reduced to piles of unpolluted, radiation-free rubble and the world's nuclear silos have all been disabled."

Maggie's hand trembled, and tea sloshed over the rim of her cup. She leapt to her feet, spinning around the kitchen in a burst of joy. "Yes! Way to go! Way-to-go! You go! girl!" she cheered, her laughter echoing through the cottage.

"Oops Lori, hope I didn't wake you. Let's have another cuppa."

The flags had been lowered, the transcripts archived, and the last envoy had returned home. In the outer provinces, children recited the new articles of unity as part of their morning lessons. Across the seas, former rivals exchanged envoys, not arms. And in the heart of the capital, beneath the great dome where the Irenic Principal had first been declared, a single light burned through the night. A quiet vigil for the idea that peace, though fragile, could be forged into permanence.

The world had not shifted in a single, blinding instant. And yet, it had shifted. Subtly, irrevocably. Her work, too, had evolved. No longer was Jessica merely a mythologist, a keeper of stories, now she was something more, something unnamed, a vessel for new understanding, a bearer of the possible. And for now, that was enough.

On Jessica's helipad, Jason Wells stands with a small case in hand. A Huey Cobra helicopter waits behind him, rotor blades spinning. Jessica approaches, wrapped in a deep burgundy cardigan. The wind tugs gently at her hair.

"My work is done here," Wells says with a wry smile. "You're still alive. And I've been reassigned."

Jessica smiles faintly. "And I was just starting to like you."

"I *am* an acquired taste."

Without warning, Jessica steps forward and kisses him. It's brief, but sincere. She steps back, eyes shining. "You're a good man, Jason Wells."

"Go forth and save the planet… again." He chuckles.

She turns to walk away, laughing, but he calls after her. "Is this the beginning of the end? Or the end of the beginning?"

She pauses, looking back. "It just is. Neutrinos, Jason, and our eternal universal consciousness are one with Creation."

Understanding passes between them. Wells places his right hand over his heart, then clasps both hands together and bows his head. Jessica mirrors the gesture.

Wells steps into the chopper and it lifts off, rising into the painted sky.

Jessica stands on the lawn alone, looking to the ocean. The wind stirs the trees. She walks to a bed of flowers, kneels, and breathes in their scent. A breeze catches her cardigan and she pulls it tighter around her, then turns to the last light of the sun beyond the horizon.

She looks up. A soft smile plays on her lips as she observes a kestrel soaring high above her. She wanted to be there with it, soaring high and there she was. She felt the breath leave her, not in fear, but in release as though something ancient within her had finally exhaled. The edges of her body dissolved like mist at sunrise. She was no longer confined to skin and bone. She was awareness, pure, unbound, and luminous.

Time slowed, then ceased. She rose not upward, but inward into a vastness that had no direction and yet held everything. Below her, the world appeared not smaller, but more beautiful, as if seen through the eyes of love itself. She saw her body resting in stillness, but she was not separate from it. She was the breath between moments, the stillness between thoughts.

A presence, gentle, radiant and familiar surrounded her. It was not a being, but a knowing. It spoke without words: *You were never only this form. You are the breath of peace, the silence behind sound, the light behind the eyes.*

Tears formed, though she had no eyes to cry. She understood. Not just intellectually, but completely. The peace she had sought was not a destination, it had always been within her, waiting to be remembered.

And in that moment, Jessica smiled not with lips, but with her soul.

Her planet receded, a glowing ember adrift in the vast tapestry of space. Soon it was just a speck among the swirling galaxies. One world among twelve, each orbiting an enormous, burning sun. And further still, that sun itself became but one in another ring of twelve, circling an even more immense and radiant star, each layer dissolving into the next, until all distinctions faded into the infinite. She was there.

The same voice, deep and resonate, spoke again without words. *Remember that you chose to come this time in order for you to experience the magnificence and the perfection of Creation. Knowing that you are that which creates life, and that which is life you are. You-Are-One. One conscious being—eternally.*

She looked and her gossamer life form was there. *Let's drift back to Earth,* she thought. *Time to go home.*

*The End
And the Beginning*

*Fiction the Precursor of Fact...
The questions may still linger.*

Acknowledgements and Reflections

It's remarkable to look back and trace the path that brought *Irenic Principal* into being. What began as an idea a story about time travel, consciousness, and truth has evolved over more than forty-five years into the screenplay and now the book you hold in your hands.

It all started with a conversation. I remember Prem Rawat, then just 17, sharing an idea with me a story of traveling back in time to meet, in every age, the Master of Truth. Then into the future: but unable to return. That seed became the foundation for the first draft of a story.

Many years later, at a party in Hollywood, I overheard three young men talking and asked if they were scientists. I shared the premise of my story, where a scientist had discovered how to collect and enhance consciousness, something Washington believed to be the ultimate deterrent.

The very next day, I received a call from Charles Stevens, a leading scientist at Livermore. He was intrigued and flew down to meet me. Over lunch, I said, "Consciousness permeates everything." He replied, "So do neutrinos millions pass through your body every second." I responded, "What if neutrinos *are* consciousness?" He went quiet, then said, "Alan, I am yours. You must be eighty years ahead."

That moment changed everything. I flew up to Livermore with my son Rowan and witnessed extraordinary experiments within the walled compound. Charles later returned my script, enriched with technical details. Charles Eric Johnston who became a lifetime close friend until his passing began to help me outline the script then titled "Ultimately Man'.

The same day I printed it, my daughter Ella called. She had just read a book I'd given her, and in the preface, Arthur C. Clarke wrote: *"The day they discovered neutrinos was the countdown to Doomsday."* She added, "Dad, three scientists also just won the Nobel Prize for discovering neutrinos."

Later, on the very day I submitted the script to DreamWorks, scientists announced that neutrinos contain mass. Possibly the Holy Grail of the universe. Six months later, the script was returned with a kind letter: they liked it, but it wasn't the right time. Still, the journey continued.

Inspired by the strength and depth of female actors, I decided to rewrite the story for a female lead. Charles's son, Brian, joined me. We tweaked and polished it until it felt right. Then, it sat on a shelf waiting, perhaps, for its moment.

In 2003, I had three readings with my dear friend Carol C. Wilson, a great seer. Those three sessions became the foundation for my book *Conversations with Einstein.* Many of the insights from those readings are woven into this story.

Later, Robert Aloha, a great author of many books and the editor of my memoir *The Empty Stage,* offered to work on the screenplay. He brought a fresh perspective, preserving the essence while enhancing the narrative. His contribution was invaluable.

To all those who have supported this project over the years. Thank you. To Katy Haber, who read most of the drafts and, upon seeing the final version, said, "Alan, this is it. Can I send it to Ridley?" Your encouragement meant the world.

And then, guess what? I started to write *The Irenic Principle: Fiction, the Precursor of Fact.*

Life unfolds in mysterious and beautiful ways. This book is a testament to that. To the power of ideas, the generosity of friends and the persistence of vision.

And to my dear Lifelong Friends. You all know who you are. Thank you for being there in all this world of love and chaotic nonsensical Earth's pain.

'In it but not of it.'
With gratitude,
Alan

ABOUT THE AUTHOR

Alan Roderick-Jones is foremost an artist whose work spans five decades across the world of film. He is the recipient of numerous awards in production design, including 4 Cleo Awards, the Silver Lion at Cannes, the New York Advertising Award for Excellence in Art Direction, and in 2017 The Oceanside International Film Festival Lifetime Achievement Award for Contribution to the World of Film Design.

His early work includes 26 features — two of which, *Star Wars* and *Nicolas & Alexandra,* garnered Academy Awards for Art Direction.

He enjoys exploring new mediums and availing himself to unique challenges. In 2003 he completed designing the interactive game environments of *The Lord of the Rings, Van Helsing, Dirty Harry,* and *Hulk 2* for Universal Vivendi Interactive Division; and "Land of Legends" for Warner Interactive.

As an artist, Alan is known in the architectural community for design of exclusive private residences. Working alongside Production Designer Donald Ashton, he co-designed the details of hotel interiors across the globe — most notably, the Mandarin in Hong Kong and the Sheratons in Cairo and Bangkok. His works of fine art reside in the collections of international collectors.

In Alan's memoir, *The Empty Stage,* he writes.

> "There is a rhythm of Life — unfolding within the eternal un-spoken silence of Creation. Yet within the silence throughout the vast Universe there is a sound — the sound we can hear within when all thoughts cease — cease — Stillness — a silent heartbeat — there Creation reveals her Divinity to us — she and we are one.

Alan Roderick-Jones has written three other books, *The Empty Stage, Conversations with Einstein,* and *Oh! Teddy O* and *the Joy of Life,* an illustrated children's book.